I MARCHED WITH SHERMAN

Ira Blanchard's Civil War World

I Marched With
SHERMAN

Civil War Memoirs of the 20th Illinois Volunteer Infantry

Ira Blanchard

J.D. Huff and Company
San Francisco

Published by J.D. Huff and Company
1032 Broadway
San Francisco

Copyright ©1992 by J.D. Huff and Company

Library of Congress Cataloging-in-Publication Data

Blanchard, Ira., b. 1835.
I marched with Sherman: Civil War memoirs of the 20th Illinois Volunteer Infantry/Ira Blanchard. -- 1st ed.
p. cm.
Includes index.

1. Blanchard, Ira, b. 1835. 2. United States. Army. Illinois Infantry Regiment, 20th (1861-1865) 3. United States -- History -- Civil War, 1861-1865 -- Regimental histories. 4. United States -- History -- Civil War, 1861-1865 -- Personal narratives. 5. Illinois -- History -- Civil War, 1861-1865 -- Regimental histories. 6. Illinois -- History -- Civil War, 1861-1865 -- Personal narratives. 7. Soldiers -- Illinois -- Biography. I. Title.
E505.5 20th.B53   1992
973.7'473 -- dc20   91-39525

ISBN: 0-9630274-5-X

Jacket Photography by Robert Alfred Brooks

Jacket Design by Nancy Ann Nichols

Printed in the United States of America

CONTENTS

CONTENTS

CONTENTS

INTRODUCTION

In April of 1934, John Nichols, then President of Idaho State University, was writing his remembrances of serving in World War I. His mother, Esther Connor Nichols, recalled that her great uncle, Ira Blanchard, had written his remembrances of serving in the Civil War. Esther's mother, Charlotte Blanchard Connor, was Ira's niece.

Thinking that John would find Ira Blanchard's work interesting, Esther wrote to her cousin, Ruth Dutton McLaughlin, who had a copy of the memoirs, and asked that she send it to John.

John had the memoirs transcribed. Upon his death in 1972, he left the work to his son, Alan Nichols. The family has no other information on Ira Blanchard other than what he had chosen to record.

What follows is an exact copy of the 1934 transcript. Except for obvious typographical errors, no changes have been made. In instances where there is a question as to exact spelling, punctuation or grammar, the Publisher has chosen to adhere to the original work rather than insert modern usage. Use of underlines, paragraph breaks and capitalization remains as it is in Blanchard's original. It is the intent of the Publisher to present not only a view of the Civil War, but the language of the time and the spirit of the author.

The Index has been added. Paul Krieger, who teaches Civil War history at the Hill School in Pottstown, Pennsylvania, prepared the Glossary as well as the map of Blanchard's route. Appendices I and II, however, were compiled by Ira Blanchard and were part of his original text.

Occasionally the author uses only the surname and the rank of an individual. No attempt has been made to further identify these persons. That task the Publisher leaves to the true Civil War scholar.

PREFACE

This little book is not designed to be a history of the great rebellion. It is intended to simply relate in the shortest manner possible the events I actually saw; the varied experiences I passed though while serving as a humble Sergeant of Co. "H" of the 20th Ill. Vol. Inft. which was the 1st Regiment of the 3rd Division of the 17th Army Corps.

It does not give a complete history of the Regiment but such things are related only as came under my own observation while I was with them at the front, which was about all the while save on the <u>march to the sea,</u> but then the few that remained went as a squad of mounted infantry and not as a Regiment.

At this distance of over 20 years much has been forgotten which I trust would be interesting to the reader, but I think enough has been given to give a good idea of Army life, of its hardships and toils, of its sunny places and its deep shadows while we strove on land and on sea, to preserve the unity of State and maintain the integrity of the land that gave us birth.

I. Blanchard

PRELIMINARY

Years ago I had a dream. I dreamed that over the brow of the great
South Hill which stretches along in front of the old home where I was
born; an army came surging over its brow, like an angry cloud before
summers storm.

The hill seemed to teem with humanity. From the old Mill which stands
on the stream in the valley, away up past Nelson Farmers, and to the left
far beyond the old San Baker house. To me 'twas a grand sight, though
terrible! Still I felt no cause for alarm, as Mr. Kyes and Jerome Pell
were busily engaged tearing up the bridges, to prevent their crossing the
big creek, down where we had a swimming hole. But my dream was
never finished, as most dreams are not, but was cut short by a kick from
Murray or Don, I forget which. Then I awoke.

I always felt an admiration for the beautiful cockade; and even the
"glorious fourth" was nothing to me without a horn of powder and a flag
floating from a pole. But the slickest thing of my boyish days was the
Sham Fight at the "Corners" in the days when a few feathers and a little
paint, would transform a crowd of men into a lot of howling savages -
when the towns people were out for general training - how with whoop
and yell they came out of the woods and charged on the big iron cannon

as she belched forth her wads of hay - how men were shot down, scalped and carried into the cornfield, but would soon sneak out and at it again.

Oh; the bloody, bloody battle field! If this is war, thought I, I never saw anything half so funny, and it was with the greatest sight satisfaction I planked down my two cents for a card of ginger bread at its close, and went on my way vowing that I had seen the greatest that ever fell to the lot of man to behold.

But passing the mere fancies of boyhood days; we come to the more weighty events of manhood when battles were no longer sham; when armies meet, not for sport, but in deadly conflict, and shot not for noise and show, but to kill; to maintain a principle underlying all good government, that a nation should protect itself against all foes from within and without.

The year 1861 was indeed a trying one for our Government. A gloom had settled on her fair prospects, as the clouds of war were gathering thick and fast, and men were loudly called to her support.

I profess that even then I had no desire for the realities of actual warfare. Yet I had no wife, no little ones, was twenty-six years old, and what the world would call sound in body, and why should I not go?

PART I

Off To A Real War

ENLISTING

So when the President called for 75,000 men for three months; when Ft. Sumpter had been bombarded, and the flames of patriotism and passion had risen to fever heat, when bonfires were burning in every town, and the fife and drum were heard continually on the streets calling men to enlist, they had little difficulty in persuading me to go.

I had trained under Jas. A. Coats as a "wide awake" during the Lincoln campaign, and had formed quite an attachment for the gallant Captain and the crowd that rallied to his support.

Early in April we formed a Company with "Jim" as its Commander and paraded around the streets of La Salle, wearing our blue ribbons in token of enlistment, armed with canes and sticks and receiving the highest encomiums of the populace, especially the ladies.

We continued drilling in the streets of La Salle about two weeks, boarding at the hotels and having a good time generally; but finding we could not be taken into the service for some time to come, we decided to disband.

In a few days, however, a call was issued by Gov. Yates for the formation of ten Regiments of Illinois troops, throughout the State, who would go into camp immediately, and on learning that a Company was being formed at Granville, Putnam County, under command of Capt. O. Frisbie, thither I determined to go.

On the 7th day of May, 1861, I started on foot in company with O. B. Champany, Stephen Springsted, Geo. Acklin and Hugh Slater brought up the rear later in the day, on horseback.

We reached Granville before dark and immediately enlisted. I turned the scale at 155 lbs. was five feet six inches in my stockings and could stand as hard a thump on the chest as any of them. We were quartered and fed by the good people of the town during the night, and the next morning formed in line, marched in front of a church where Scriptures were read, prayers offered, and we were ready to proceed on our journey by 8 o'clock.

THE START

This was a memorable day for the little town of Granville. Men, women and children turned out by the hundreds to see the boys off. Many came from long distances to see what they had never seen before, their husbands, fathers or brothers off to the war. The scenes at parting were truly affecting; but we from over the river having no kin or sweethearts in the crowd, did nothing but laugh save when some of the damsels would attempt to hug us. Wagons were provided to convey the boys to where they were to take the train at Peru; and hundreds followed in carriages, on horse back and on foot; so the procession was more than a mile long. Before crossing the river at Peru a halt was made, and in a grove a sumptuous lunch was given by the ladies that followed.

Then at Peru, amid the shouts of the assembled multitude and the bang of a cannon on the bluff, we took the train for Joliet, where we arrived about 4 o'clock and went directly to the Fair Grounds where several other companies had already arrived. There had been erected around the enclosure some temporary sheds or barracks which were partitioned off into small compartments capable of holding five or six soldiers each, and on the ground was scattered a little straw by way of bedding.

IN CAMP

I shall never forget our first night in camp. After partaking of our rations, consisting of a little sour bread, a slice of bacon and some coffee from a tin cup, we turned in, but not to sleep. The night was cold, a little frosty, and having no overcoats or blankets we lay and shook with the cold all night. I had slept in a warm room for the last three months on a soft feather bed, and this was indeed a change too great.

The ground was hard and damp, our quarters cramped, and if sleep dared come to our weary eyes, she was ruthlessly driven away by those who were in as great distress as we. A hooting and howling was kept up all night. Some would call to their mothers for more quilts, saying they were freezing. Others would keep up a barking like some bull dog to frighten away the night. While occasionally one would find his way to the top of the fence and begin to crow that the morning might come. In the morning we had no small difficulty in straightening out our benumbed limbs before roll call. However, we soon became accustomed to this rough mode of life, and after a few weeks began to like it quite well.

FORMATION OF REGIMENT

Ten Companies having now arrived and taken quarters, the next in order was the formation of the Regiment.

The field and staff officers were elected by ballot after an exciting canvass of two days, during which time many prominent men came to camp to urge their claims upon the boys for an office; among whom was the Hon. Owen Lovejoy, but he did not succeed.

The election resulted as follows:

Colonel	C. C. Marsh
Lieutenant Colonel	F. E. Irwin
Major	Chas. Goodwin for field.

For Staff

Adjutant	C. Field
Quartermaster	Tiffany
1 Surgeon	Goodbrake
2 Surgeon	Baley
Chaplain	Button
Sergeant Major	Archdeacon
Color Sergeant	Morley

Position of Companies

Right

Co. "A"	Capt. Woolf
Co. "C"	Capt. Richards
Co. "E"	Capt. Tunison
Co. "G"	Capt. Irwin
Co. "I"	Capt. King

Colors

Co. "H"	Capt. Frisbie
Co. "K"	Capt. Kennard
Co. "F"	Capt. Pullen
Co. "D"	Capt. Hilderbrand
Co. "B"	Capt. Barletson

Left   [This section was left blank by Ira Blanchard]

After the election and formation of the Regiment was over, we became more settled. Our quarters were greatly improved by building bunks up on one side which left us space enough to put in a wide board for a table on which we spread our "grub" which with the few extras we could buy, and with Hugh Slater to say grace, made our place quite like a home, and with our new blankets we began to feel happy.

About the first of June we received our arms (old Springfield Muskets) and was designated the 20th Reg. Ill. Vol., and remained in "Camp Goodel" about six weeks constantly drilling preparatory to active service at the front, when we were mustered into the United States service for three years.

By this time the regiment began to make quite a respectable appearance, being about 1200 strong, and we would attract large crowds when on 'dress parade' in the field near the town.

A brass band from Putnam Co. was added, which together with our Drum Corps enlivened our camp with plenty of martial music; and had it not been for the frequent attacks on the Guard House (which by the way was demolished several times) and the ungovernable spirit of the boys of Co. "A" styled "Champaign Tigers" - who insisted on tearing down the high board fence which surrounded our camp, and going on a "bum" around town - our stay at Camp Goodel would have been of great benefit, as well as quite enjoyable.

Many people came from Chicago and the surrounding country to see the newly made soldiers; and with the frequent Picnics, Shows and Glee clubs which resorted thither, there was nothing lacking to make it interesting, and we had nothing to complain of but hard drill and poor grub.

A WEDDING

A memorable event was the marriage of our Major Goodwin in true military style, who came galloping up from town one fine morning by the side of a young lady and several friends on horseback. The Regiment was hustled out on "double quick" for what purpose we knew not. Was an attack expected? Oh no, our muskets were too many for them. We formed in hollow square into which the bridal party rode, and without dismounting were made man and wife by our Chaplain Button, and went galloping back to town again amid the shouts of the boys.

FARTHER SOUTH

On the 18th day of June we were ordered to go farther South. Accordingly two trains of many cars each were placed at our disposal, and we moved down the Chicago and Alton road and were enthusiastically cheered all along the line by the crowds who gathered to see us pass.

We reached Alton the next day and went into camp back of town, where we were joined by Heckers Regiment. A regiment from Freeport and one from Peoria. This formed a Brigade which was commanded by Brig. General Pope.

Here we were supplied with new tents, and when they were all pitched along the hills the place began to look more like a military encampment. Here we continued our drill and study of tactics. And here, as in all other places, we would slip off in spite of the vigilance of the Guard, go up to Monticelo, about a mile distant, where there was a female Seminary, have a chat with the young ladies who would always insist on our coming back again. We went with a rush on the Fourth of July, on which occasion they gave us a sumptuous dinner and entertainment, our Chaplain delivering the oration.

Our next move was down to the Arsenal at St. Louis, but as there had been trouble there, our guns were loaded before our Steamer reached the landing, but we saw nothing of trouble and went into camp in the grounds of the Arsenal where our old guns were exchanged for new ones, which change we greatly appreciated. We also received knapsacks, haversacks and canteens , and when all these are full, 'tis no wonder the soldier feels more like a pack mule than anything else.

Again shipping camp equipage, arms and ammunition and all pertaining to a small army, on board the large Steamer Illinois, we began again the descent of the Mississippi farther down towards "Dixie." Just as the sun was sinking behind the western hills, our steamer rounded to in front of the beautiful and historic town of

CAPE GIRARDEAU.

As we neared the wharf, men, women and children crowded around waving hats and handkerchiefs from the streets from the upper windows of the tall buildings in token of their joy at our approach, but the stars and stripes were nowhere visible. The people were as a rule loyal; yet they had been constantly plundered, threatened by rebel bands that infested that part of the State, and now they saw their relief at hand, and rejoiced at the presence of the Yankees.

'Twas near dark before our grounds were selected and we were ready to disembark when we formed in line and moved to some open ground a little to the north of the town close by the river banks.

Here we threw our pickets, stacked our arms and pitched our tents and made ourselves at home. Learning that just before our arrival, a party claiming to belong to the rebel Prices force had entered the town and carried off several loads of provisions, a detail accordingly was sent out in hot pursuit under Col. Irwin who overtook them before they had gone many miles, recaptured the stores and returned them prisoners before morning.

Col. Marsh proceeded immediately to make all male citizens take the oath of allegiance to stop and search all vessels passing up and down the river, and no one was allowed to leave town without a pass from headquarters.

Early one morning in August a grand procession applied for admission within our lines. The head of the column was brought to a halt at the outer sentinel, while far down the road ranged a motley crowd of

Missourians on mules, in cotton wagons or on foot. These were the Scott Co. Home Guard who had been frightened away from their homes during the night and had come all the way from Scott Co. for safety within our lines. They were dressed in their native butternut and under their broad brimmed slouch hats their unkempt hair hung down upon their shoulders. To the back of each was strapped a gun and their canvas bags were filled with corn bread that they might not starve during their long journey to the Yankee Camp. Col. Marsh promptly admitted them as they were loyal citizens and when their line of mules, wagons and men had been "dressed" in front of ours, their Leader rode out in front of his men and addressed our Colonel something as follows:

Colonel, we all have left our homes, our wives, our babies and our cattle and come here to fight, bleed and die with you-uns, in the cause of liberty, in the interest of the best government the sun ever shone on, sir. We will stand by the old flag, sir, and will go into the thickest of the fight with you all, sir, in the defence of our common country, and the grand old State of Missouri, sir.

They stacked arms, took up their quarters in an old Soap Factory were fed from our commissary, and after laying around about a week went home declaring they had had enough of war.

EXPEDITION TO THE WHITEWATER

On the 17th of July Companies "E" "H" and "G" of the 20th under Capt. Richards were detached to go on an expedition into the interior to surprise and if possible capture any guerrilla bands that might be collecting in those quarters, as reports were continually coming in of their depredations on Union men who remained at home.

Taking rations for five days, filling our boxes with cartridges we moved noiselessly out of town about twelve o'clock at night, that no rebel sympathizers might learn of our departure and convey a warning to the enemy.

After a hard night's march we reached the Whitewater early the next day, took possession of the ferry, crossed over to the opposite side where we rested for an hour, partook of our "hard tack and sow belly," and was ready to push forward again. The day was extremely hot, and by this time I began to appreciate something of the hardships of a soldier. My feet were already blistered, I had had no sleep the night before, we had traveled nearly 30 miles carried a heavy knapsack, haversack, musket, and ammunition, which to have carried one mile ordinary times would make the stoutest quail, and I was almost ready to sink under the burden. But to have done so would have been dangerous in the extreme, there was nothing to do but push on, on all day and at night sleep out in the woods with naught but the blue sky above us and the cold damp ground beneath us.

Pushing boldly out perhaps 30 or 40 miles from the cape we came to a halt, as we had by this time gone as far as the original plan or as prudence would allow. Here we "bivouaced" and remained several days scouting and scouring the country in all directions, but meeting with no formidable body of armed men; yet rumors would come to us almost every hour of bands in this direction or that; but on our arrival they were not there; so when our rations became short and our work of observation thoroughly accomplished, we started on the homeward march, but not until we had made several old farmers prisoners, captured their old rusty shot guns and brought them in triumph as trophies of war.

Again in camp our duties of drill, "guard mount" and patrolling the town were resumed. A bakery had been improvised in the old Soap Factory, with Sam Forbes as baker, and we were now supplied with an abundance of "soft bread" which with the large supply of fruit that found its way into our camp made our tables quite enjoyable.

Then the native population were so very kind to the Yankees, their houses were always open to bid them welcome, and it is no wonder that many of the boys desired to "fight it out on that line if it did take all summer."

We were now joined by the 8th Missouri Inft. under Col. Smith, and soon other troops arrived from the North; our strength at the Cape was now over 6000.

"PIRATE LUELLA"

An old steamer was seized a few miles below and brought to camp. She had been used as a ferry in times of peace, but was capable of floating only about twenty men. However, the old thing was tinkered up as best they could, and Capt. Pullen took command as "Commodore" which title he retained among the boys as long as he was with the Army. The stars and stripes were run up at the mast head and blood red streamers floated to the breeze, and when the brave Pullen had mounted the deck, she was ready for war. The crowd collected on the shore to see the start. Finally the signal was given, the steam let on - the old thing gave a lurch, her wheel went around two or three times, then stopped.

"Come ahead on her John," sang out the Commodore from above. But she stood like a horse that all the coaxing and whipping could not start. Finally after a little fixing, a full head of steam was turned on when the wheel flew so rapidly and she struck down the stream so swiftly, that the Commodore thought she would be shipwrecked - cried loudly to his engineer, "Stop her, John, stop her;" then came back shouts of laughter from the crowd on shore, and the Commodore swore he would get out of sight before he would try the gol darn thing again. However, the thing got to going quite well and we had lots of fun with her floating up and down the river robbing peach orchards or looking after the "rebs."

ARMY DISCIPLINE

Our post here had now grown to one of great importance, and all things were done in true military style. 'Twas here that some of the most severe punishments were meeted out for disobedience of orders, only a few of which I will mention. The <u>Buck</u> and <u>Gag</u> was first resorted to by Col. Marsh in punishing an unruly soldier of Co. A. This was done by binding a large piece of wood in the victim's mouth, thus keeping the mouth wide open, then tying the hands firmly together, then compelling the victim to sit on the ground, draw the knees up under the chin, and a long stick thrust in between the knees and elbows, thus keeping him doubled up with mouth wide open three or four hours at a time.

"Drumming out of Camp," is another mode of punishment in case a man is too ugly to be a soldier. His head is shaved, his hands tied behind him, then the entire post is drawn up in hollow square, and he is compelled to march around this square with six bayonets pointing at his back while the band plays the "rogues march." This is considered the most disgraceful punishment that can be inflicted.

Hanging by the thumbs, is another mode and is next to shooting. This was the penalty a young man paid at the Cape for refusing to obey the orders of Gen. Prentiss. He was tied with strong cords around the wrists which were passed up over the limb of a tree, then he was hauled up so that his toes would just touch the ground. In this position he hung until his arms and face were turned black and his tongue protruded from his mouth.

During the months of July and August we were kept in a constant state of excitement from reports from the Reb. Jeff Thompson, who, it was rumored, was collecting a large force in the interior of the State, with the avowed determination of dislodging us from the soil of Missouri and many a night we were hustled out and into line on the supposition that the foe was near at hand.

On the 15 of August, Gen. Prentiss, who was then in command at Cairo, sent word that a large force had passed around Bird's Point on their way north, and would probably strike at the Cape and try and dislodge us. He also sent a battery of light artillery to our assistance.

On the night of the 16th it really began to look as though a "brush" with the enemy was imminent. Refugees began to come in to town who reported them at Jackson, a town sixteen miles out, and rapidly advancing.

Accordingly strong outposts were stationed on all the commanding positions. Guns and ammunitions were made ready, lines formed and awaited the signal from the pickets, commissary stores were all packed and put aboard the army wagons, ready for removal as events should render necessary. Tents were "struck" and carried to a hill a little back of the town.

On this hill we took a position in a semi-circle, piling up our tents in front of us by way of breast works. Here we remained all night watching and waiting, but no enemy came; not a gun was fired. Perhaps the "Rebs" had changed their minds and thought we were too strong for them, or perhaps there was no enemy at all, which I have always thought was nearest the truth. However, we kept on expecting them, for in the morning all hands were put to work with pick and shovel, and in a few days the hill was crowned with a strong line of breastworks, and every little hill was converted into a rifle pit. Then six large siege guns arrived from St. Louis and were put in position. Then a flag staff was erected on which the stars and stripes were run up, which gave the place the appearance of a strong fortress where we could bid defiance to all rebeldom should they appear.

THE "CONISTOGA"

A few days later a gun boat, one of the first built, came steaming up the river. Her black sides, frowning port-holes, and blood red streamers, were things hideous to behold. Yet she caused general rejoicing in our camp as she floated the stars and stripes, telling unmistakably that she was on our side. She rounded to at the landing, then fired a few shots from her bow guns just to show how cleverly she could deliver her 67 lb. shell. Then our battery on the hill opened up, and bang, bang, went the guns from the parapet, and bang, bang, went the guns of the Conistoga, by way of an answering salute. Then the bands struck up and music and cheering was mingled with the roar of artillery, which was kept up for hours; but as her mission was to patrol the rivers she did not remain with us long. After banqueting some of the officers on board, she steamed away. Leaving a strong garrison at the Cape, all the available forces under Gen. Pope, were moved to

JACKSONVILLE,

a strong secession town of 2000 inhabitants, sixteen miles west from the river. We had little difficulty in entering the town and soon had our flag floating from the dome of the Court House. Here we were joined by the forces of Gen. Prentiss, consisting of the 15th, 17th, 19th, and 22nd Ill. Regiments, together with the 22nd Iowa, and Bewells flying Artillery and a part of the 1st Ill. Cavalry. We saluted them with eleven guns on entering the town, and when tents were pitched all over the fields, the place presented a truly war-like appearance; as this was the largest force I had yet seen together. Here I found many acquaintances among the boys of Col. Stewart's 19th Regiment, and we passed a very pleasant week during our stay at this place.

But Gen. Prentiss moved his forces on in their work of scouring the country as far as Iron Mountain, and after ransacking the town and country around for arms and contraband of war, we again went back to the Cape with large amount of stores and drove of negroes.

But we halted not at the Cape. Taking transports on the 10th we again, with bag and baggage, bade farewell to the beautiful Cape, its beautiful houses, its beautiful women and steamed farther down the Mississippi to

BIRDS POINT.

Landing on the 11th, we went into camp inside of a position which had already been fortified across the river from Cairo on the Missouri side. The country around is low and there are large Cyprus swamps to the west and south, and it is no wonder that a great many of the boys became sick, and soon the field hospitals became crowded. Yet the work of thorough drill was kept up, and often scouting parties were sent into the country, as rebel bands were continually prowling around.

Yet as for me, I was not long at this place before I became sick with
what the surgeons called Rumt. Fever. I lay in my tent for several days,
during which time I had taken an incredible amount of quinine, but grew
rapidly worse, when our Regiment was called suddenly away to go in
pursuit of Jeff Thompson. I was taken with the remaining sick ones on
board a fast steamer to

MOUND CITY.

Here the Government had established a large Military Hospital, being
an accessible point on the Ohio River six miles above Cairo on the
Illinois side. Here were a great many sick soldiers, and the number of
deaths were about six per day. I lingered for about four weeks before
any change for the better took place, witnessing many sad scenes of
suffering and death, which I have not space in this book to enumerate.
Many of my own Company were there, a part of whom died, others went
home as incurable; but on the whole I considered the care and attention
we received from Surgeons and nurse good for an Army Hospital.

A few days after our arrival we were informed that the 20th Regiment
had come up with the Rebel Jeff Thompson at Fredricks Town and after
a sharp skirmish had routed his band and taken many prisoners and had
got back to Birds Point without the loss of a single man.

A little later Gen. Grant moved a force down the right bank of the river
to a point opposite Columbus called Bellmont, where the rebels attacked
and tried to surround him and after a sharp fight withdrew with all his
killed and wounded. These were brought to our Hospital, the first batch
of wounded soldiers I had ever seen, and carefully attended by the
Surgeons, most of whom soon recovered and were able to be about
again, and they would relieve somewhat the monotony by relating
incidents of the fight.

I began to convalesce after a four week's stay at the Hospital and was
able to walk about and sit at the long table during meals, and many a
time chum Smith and I would slip off to some farmer's house and get

the lady to cook us a chicken, or something better than we could get at the Hospital table. One young man went out one day and got what the boys called "a square meal" but ate too much, and he was not well enough. He came back, said he would lie down a bit and take a rest. He lay very quiet. In a little while we went to tell him supper was ready, when we found him dead. Another, a little luney, imagined he could not recover unless he went to his regiment, but was not allowed to go. Finally by some means or other he got out, slipped the guard and was found next day in the woods, half-way to Cairo, dead.

In a few weeks more I was pronounced able to join my regiment, a thing I had longed for some days. Accordingly I resumed my duties again at the point with my regiment, but found I was not strong, though comparatively well. So sleeping on the ground in a tent was a little severe, and it seemed some times I would give out again; but as colder weather came on and the air became purer, I had no serious draw-back, and could soon eat as hearty of "hard-tack" and "sow belly" as any of them.

'Twas now October; we bad been several times out along the Charlestown Railroad; had captured an engine and some cars with which we were enabled to run with ease 8 or 10 miles out into the Swamps where large details were put to work and loading logs on the cars with which to build barrack or winter quarters.

Our arms we always took along as there was great danger from Guerrilla Bands who constantly hovered as near our camps as prudence would allow in hopes of capturing those who should stray off too far. Once they made a dash on our guard at the large bridge in the swamp run them off and burned it before help could arrive, thus preventing our running our train as far west as Charlestown. So while a portion of the men were at work others would be at work standing guard, hunting in the forest, or gathering the delicious Pecans as they fell from the lofty trees which grew there in abundance. Thus besides our train of logs and shingles we seldom came in without a good supply of game. But the palm was taken by young Smith of our Company who brought down a huge Buck, which supplied our "mess" with venison for several days.

Our old engine was a poor concern, and some times it was with great difficulty we could get her to go at all, and many times during a trip all hands would have to dismount and bring water in pails to get up steam enough to get her to crawl along.

WINTER QUARTERS

We worked faithfully, however, and before the first snow fell, we had our quarters up and ready to occupy. These consisted of ten long log buildings for the rank and file, one for each Company. These were divided into ten compartments, each being supplied with a huge fire-place at one end, the Captain and wife occupying the first, the Orderly Sergeant the next, and so on through the row, a Sergeant with each squad of men. Then at right angles with the Company rows and a little distant from them, was a long building for the general officers, such as Colonel, Lieutenant Colonel, Major, Chaplain, Quartermasters, Surgeons, etc.

On one side of the mens quarters were erected bunks one above the other, which with a little straw and our blankets made quite a cozy place to sleep. On the other side was a long bench over which was our gunrack. Then we had a table, a few stools, and had you looked in of a cold night when our big blazing fire was roaring and cracking you would have said "surely there is happiness in that place." One night we would have a prayer-meeting, the next would be devoted to cards and such amusements, and perhaps the next, if Dixon and Dock got together there would be a fight. On the whole there was a jolly set of boys in those winter quarters as one would wish to see. The following is a specimen of one of the many songs which might have been heard day or night had you been there.

> "My name it is Jo Bowers
> I have a brother Ike
> I came from old Missouri
> All the way from Pike.
> I'll tell you why I left there

And how I came to roam,
And leave my poor old mother
So far away from home."

Thus the cold winter passed quite merrily, save when we had to be out on guard or hunting stray secesh which would occur quite often.

CHARLESTOWN, MO.

On about the 10th of January, 1862, our officers thought they would lay a trap and bag some rebel cavalry that frequently came up from the south to Charlestown, a small town twelve miles southwest from Birds Point. On learning that they were in camp at that place, a force of cavalry was sent out just at dark to make a wide detour to the North but close in on the town at daylight the next morning while the infantry was to go out by the Railroad as far as the burned bridge, then make its way through the cyprus swamps, move up by the Columbus road and strike the town at daylight from the South. Accordingly a strong force with 40 rounds of ammunition and three days rations left camp about 10 o'clock at night, moved by the Railroad as far as the burned bridge. The night was dark as Egypts and when we entered the Cyprus Swamp we could not see a hand before us. To pass through there by day was extremely dangerous as from the cyprus roots sharp "knees" spring up, which taper to a sharp point at the top as keen as the point of a bayonet, and if one should stumble and fall on one of these it would be almost certain death. So we each strapped our guns to our backs, each took a fire brand in his right hand, which by swinging at his feet could see where to step while with the other he would hold on to his file leader. Thus in single file, and with great difficulty, we worked our way through this dismal place, then passing through some fields, we at length struck the main road far to the south of the town about 3 o'clock.

Here our ranks were reformed, and the different Regiments allowed to "close up," then we began a rapid march towards the town. As we passed a house on the road I noticed that the people were astir and bright lights were burning. This looked suspicious to me; but as the officer saw nothing wrong in this, why should I? At any rate, the column moved on and never slackened its pace. Again I noticed that from the chimney of that same house large sparks came flying out as though something unusual had been thrown on the fire. Then almost instantly came a volley of musketry from whence I could not see, but the bullets flew thick and fast. Then the whole line commenced firing into the woods, the fields, anywhere, but we could see nothing in the darkness save the flash at the ends of our guns. Some broke and ran and vowed they heard heavy masses of cavalry moving rapidly off. A fight so unexpected so long before light was more than we had bargained for. In fact we had run into an ambuscade, and the very ones that we expected to trap had trapped us, or at least had given us a severe volley and rode off with every man, while we were left with six killed outright, and with twenty badly wounded. We did not move farther that night but stood in a drenching rain until daylight; then gathered up our dead and wounded and moved back to camp as best we could, having made an utter failure.

But we were not allowed to remain in our snug quarters long. The weather was cold and altogether unsuited to campaigning, yet it would not do to let so large a force as was at Birds Point be idle. The life and spirit of an army depends on its activity, so to learn the strength of the enemy in the towns to the southwest, another

EXPEDITION

was planned to reconnoiter along the line of the Texas and Cairo Railroad which had now been repaired so we could run a train 20 miles beyond Charlestown. So about the 20th of January a large force of Cavalry and Infantry set out along this road with rations for six days, with instructions to penetrate as far as possible into the interior and break up any armed bands that might be found. The Infantry went out by railroad and encamped at Charlestown, while the cavalry moved farther on by two different roads. The next day we pushed on 30 miles farther and went into a camp at a place called Burtrand. From this point our progress was slow, as we had to go on foot, and we soon entered another Cyprus Swamp through which only the Railroad ran, and the "Rebs" had burned most of the trestle work on which the road was built, and over this we had to crawl some times on our hands and knees or shove ourselves along on a single rail that reached from span to span.

Weary and faint we entered Sykestown about 9 o'clock at night with the rain pouring down in torrents, and as the night was extremely dark, we went into camp. The boys built fires in the streets and made coffee. Then we broke open the stores and shops and crawled into whatever place we could find, and thus passed the night. When I awoke in the morning, I found I had slept on the counters of a Dry Goods store.

Our work of scouring the country continued about five days, during which time we captured some stores of provisions, but finding the towns almost wholly deserted and meeting no armed men, we returned again to the Point after a long and tedious march.

DEMONSTRATION AGAINST COLUMBUS

was next in order. So after a few days rest we embarked on steamers and dropped down the river to within ten miles of Columbus, while the gun boats went down and engaged the batteries of that strong hotel. We landed on the left bank and our Brigade was left to hold the landing, while a strong force was sent to the southeast to destroy all the railroads leading into that place, thus cutting them off from their main source of supplies. We remained at this landing a little more than a week, and called the place Ft. Jefferson, but before we left our supply of rations ran out and there were loud cries of "bread or blood" throughout the camp before we left. The expedition having accomplished the work of destroying we again moved back to our quarters.

But these unimportant events, though much talked of at the time, seem as mere trifles compared with the more exciting ones which occurred later on. In fact war with us had not really begun, yet all these manoeuvres were of the utmost importance to properly discipline and prepare the soldier to endure hardships and privations; to weed out the weak ones and give skill in the use of arms which are his constant companions.

On the first of February a large fleet of Transports were collected at Cairo and Paducah to convey the troops further down into "Dixie" and by the stir and bustle about headquarters we all understood that something was going to happen.

On loading one of the large steamers it was the bad luck of a poor mule to fall overboard into the river as he was being forced up the gang plank much against his will. He went under several times and many thought he would soon drown and 'twould be useless to attempt his rescue. However a rope was let down with a noose which was soon worked over his neck. Then a crowd sprang to the rope and Mr. Mule was landed up the steep bank with his tongue protruding from his mouth, more dead than alive. Then some one yelled to the teamster "Here's your mule" and always after if any one was seen about the army looking for anything, some one was sure to shout "Here's your mule." When the mule was well on shore and the halter taken off he had to be helped to his feet, but when well on his feet he backed up to another mule that was looking on, and let his heels fly as though nothing had happened.

PART II

Into The Thick Of It

CAPTURE OF HENRY

When all the available troops at Birds Point, Cairo and Paducah were in readiness and placed on board the transports, together with all necessary stores for the sustenance of a large army, we moved up the Ohio River on the 3rd to the mouth of the Tennessee where we were joined by the forces at Paducah when we began the ascent of the latter stream.

The first day was stormy, raining and snowing all the time, and Dick Ogelsby, who was in charge of our boats, insisted that the rank and file should remain out on deck, storm or no storm, while the officers had a good time within. But the cabin with its warm fire, was too inviting; so we pressed on "Dick" and his guards from all quarters, and some vowed they would throw him overboard if he did not submit. Finally the haughty Colonel yielded, and we went in out of the cold filling the cabin so full there was scarcely room to move, and had a comfortable time the rest of the way. This was our first victory.

By the night of the 4th we were well up the river and nearing the State line where we expected to meet with opposition, and it now became necessary to move with caution. Finding a landing the troops disembarked on the left bank of the river and encamped for night; while the fleet of Gun Boats under Capt. Porter took up a position farther up the stream.

Then the "Jessie Scouts" a squad of six young men who were specially trained for the business, were sent out to spy out the enemy's strength and position, but finding the Fort at too great a distance and nothing being learned, we again boarded our transport and moved farther up stream.

By this time all eyes were intent on seeing the rebel colors in the distance. The Gun Boats moved four abreast in advance. The shores were closely watched for masked batteries, and on seeing five or six men watching us in front of an old house, Capt. Porter let fly a shell from the "Benton" and they fled to the woods in all directions. When within two miles of the Fort, it being nearly night, another halt was made, and all the troops went ashore, together with the light artillery, preparatory to an attack by land and water at the same time. On the morning of the 6th we made our coffee early, and after inspection of boxes were ready to move. Colonel Marsh lit a fresh cigar as he sat laxily on his horse, and asked if we could charge bayonets.

Captain Porter's fleet was fast getting up steam, and running up the blood red streamers, the large guns were loaded and ammunition placed convenient. The fleet sending up her clouds of black smoke and dressed for war, looked terrific.

By eight o'clock all was in readiness, and the army moved out by a rapid march leaving the fleet to its own fate in the river while we made a detour of a mile or so to strike the Fort in the rear. But looking back to the river, we could see the fleet already in motion. Captain Porter was evidently getting impatient. Soon we could hear the boom of the big guns of the Fort. The fleet steamed steadily up; then they opened at short range and the roar became terrific. Shells flew in all directions or burst high in the air, while we were doing our best to reach the rear of the Fort. For half an hour the thunder of the artillery had continued. Captain Porter had pushed the "Benton" right up to the guns of the enemy, putting in his broad-sides thick and fast and sending death and destruction before her, when a shell enters her port hole and she drifts helpless down the stream.

All at once the fire slackens - a courier soon arrives saying the Fort had surrendered and the rebel colors hauled down. With a shout all went on "double quick" for the Fort, but we arrived a little too late, as most of the Garrison had fled. General Tilman, the Commander, had given up his sword to Captain Porter, and the stars and stripes had been run up on their flag staff. We then stacked arms and eagerly looked over the scene of the 'fray.' The Fort was built on a bend of the river in an admirable position, mounting several guns of heavy caliber. Around the Fort proper was a line of earth works enclosing about ten acres. In the parapets next the river we found several bodies that had been literally torn to pieces. Legs, arms and heads were scattered in all directions by the bursting of shell from the fleet. One of the large guns had been dismounted and one burst. The few survivors who were left in the Fort declared that Satan himself could not withstand such a torrent.

We rested here for a few days, during which time we were strongly reinforced and a large amount of supplies collected preparatory to another move against Donaldson on the Cumberland River about fourteen miles distant. During our stay the gun boats pushed farther up the Tennessee, and destroyed the large bridge of the Nashville and Chattanooga Railroad, and penetrated as far as the Mussle Shoals near the Alabama line.

FORT DONALDSON

On the morning of the 10th the entire army was again in motion. We moved about ten miles the first day by several different routes, through a rough and heavily timbered country, taking heavy supplies of ammunition and rations. Before night we had encountered some cavalry and run them off with little difficulty. The next day we came in sight of the Fort and moved with utmost caution. All day was spent in taking positions from hill to hill as we gradually closed in on the strong hold. Picket posts were encountered and driven in; occasionally we would unsling knapsacks and rush up a hill to secure some commanding position; and on the night of the 12th we slept within range of their outer parapets, on a cold frosty night, without our coffee, and no fires to warm our weary and benumbed bodies.

This night to me was a gloomy one as I lay and shook with the cold until daylight. I cared not so much what would come on the morrow, but the present suffering, who could endure it without a murmur. But such we must endure if we would be a soldier; and I saw no help for it; if we should kindle a fire, it would only be to invite a shell from the enemy into our midst, and at the same time give the enemy a better idea of our position and strength.

The morning of the 13th opened clear and somewhat warmer. The field batteries opened from our position, by throwing a few shells into the enemies works, but finding the distance too great, ceased until a nearer approach could be made. We then moved farther to the right upon a ridge road, leading into the town of Donaldson, upon which we fought our way until within 20 rods of the outer works. From this ridge we had a commanding view of their works for nearly a mile. At our left was a low stretch of cleared land, rising to the top of the hill on which the enemies rifle pits were built. In front of these pits they had felled all the scrub oaks, and sharpened their branches in such a manner that it was extremely difficult for men to pass through.

It was in this clearing that the first real demonstration was made. About 8 o'clock several regiments were massed under cover of the woods below and started with colors flying up the hill. It was a beautiful sight to behold from our position on the ridge. Every eye was strained to catch a glimpse of this heroic band. We cheered them heartily as they met unflinchingly the galling fire from above. On, on they pressed, meeting and returning volley after volley until within a few feet of the redoubts, when becoming entangled in the "abettis" they could make no farther progress, when they withdrew bringing their wounded with them. The remainder of the day was spent in skirmishing and thoroughly investigating the place. Our position that night was about fifteen rods from their outer works behind a rise of ground which afforded a partial protection only as we crouched down to the ground. This was covered with scrub oaks but not dense enough to impede the progress of troops. Beyond this thicket the ground sloped for a few rods, then rose again as it neared their works. This depression was also covered with fallen trees with sharp pointed boughs rendering it almost impossible for troops to work through with any kind of order.

On our right was the 11th Illinois, while on our left was the 16th Wisconsin with their favorite Eagle "Old Abe" while just beyond the 16th was Taylor's Battery supported by Burgis Sharp Shooters, which as the ground lay was all the troops immediately in sight; but judging from the size of their works, our lines must have been more than three miles long.

During the night we stood at arms most of the time. A heavy skirmish line lay a few rods in front of us, which kept up a constant firing all night, and there was no time that the bullets from the Fort could not be heard spinning past.

Occasionally a few at a time would slip back to the rear, and in a ravine make a little coffee or roast a slice of bacon on a stick, but during this we would generally have to jump back to our arms two or three times before we were able to get a bite. This state of siege continued during the 14th. We had the place now thoroughly invested and held them as with an iron grip, waiting for the fleet of gun boats to arrive before moving on their works. At 11 o'clock we knew by the booming of heavy guns that they were already engaging the batteries on the river; but no advance was made by the land forces.

We could not see the fleet from our position, but could hear the huge shells burst as they flew thick and fast from the iron monsters which were steaming up nearer and nearer the Fort. This heavy firing was kept up about two hours; then all at once it ceased. We could see by the smoke that the Gun Boats were falling back down the river. Two pilots had been killed, and the boats greatly disabled.

Then came a tremendous shout from the rebel line. The gun boats were whipped. Some even dared to raise their head above their breastworks and yell across to us, "Now come on, you d____d blue bellied yankees; we are ready for you now. We can lick all the Yankees in God's creation." The danger which threatened them from the river was now past, and they now imagined they had only to fight the Yankees from a safe position from behind their breast works.

Night at last came on, and with it, rain, sleet and snow. It also became much colder. Our over-coats being wet, froze stiff upon us, so 'twas with difficulty we could bend our bodies, and we had to stamp our feet, rub our hands and dance about to keep from freezing. Besides the "Rebs" were becoming extremely annoying; they were popping away at us all the time, and we did not know what moment they would come out and pounce upon us; so we did not take off our boxes or leave our arms the entire night.

Colonel Marsh would say when the firing would become unusually heavy, "Boys now <u>dont</u> let them drive you off," to which they would all respond, "<u>Never.</u>"

All night long we could hear them at work inside, strengthening their works, hauling up guns with oxen, and placing them in position in our front, and everything pointed to lively work in the morning.

BATTLE OF THE 15TH

The morning opened clear and cold. Everything along the line was in readiness; yet we had stood at arms the entire night, with but little food and greatly fatigued, yet ready for any duty that should devolve upon us.

Soon after daylight the rebel Artillery opened briskly all along their line. We crouched down close to the ground, to let the storm of grape and canister pass, which was then sweeping through the trees and tearing off the boughs at a fearful rate. Taylor's Battery replied with spirit at times; but the gunners were often forced away from their guns to seek shelter behind trees until a little lull would occur, when they would up and at it with all their might, making the balls fly thick and fast into the enemies works as the boys encouraged them with cheer upon cheer. During this fierce cannonade, Colonel W. H. L. Wallace, who was in command of our Brigade rode slowly along the lines with single orderly, as cool as though he was a thousand miles from an enemy - never dodging or looking around, while the shells were bursting and tearing up the ground close to his horse's feet.

Following this fierce cannonade, came the sound of musketry up to our right. Our Regiment stood up and made ready. The line was as perfect as on dress parade. Colonel Marsh sat on his black horse twenty paces to the rear, Lt. Col. Irwin on a noble bay to the right, and Major Richards to the left. Our hands were numb with the cold, but what of that? The hot blood was beginning to tingle in every vein; in fact our blood was up. Boxes were opened, bayonets set. Nearer and nearer came the rattle of musketry. Now Colonel Irwin shouts, "They're coming!! in solid column." "For God's sake don't let them drive you off," shouted Colonel Marsh. At the same time the skirmish line came running back. Colonel Irwin orders them back to their position again, and says: "Give them fire! Stagger their ranks!" Which they did, but immediately fell back on the line again.

These were the last words of Colonel Irwin. He had given his last command, for just then a shell struck him, and the fine gentleman and brave officer fell from his horse a lifeless corpse.

On came the enemy. Our line stood firm, but fired not a shot until they were within five rods of us, and their coon skin caps could be seen all along in our front. Then our rear rank leveled their muskets when Marsh yelled "fire." I kept my eye on the advancing foe, and saw several of the tall fine looking fellows with coon skin caps curl up in death at the first volley, and others went limping and crawling away. Then as soon as the smoke had cleared a little the front rank fired staggering the enemy greatly, and then fire slackened for a moment. In the meantime, some of our boys had fallen. Private John McKue fell shot in his head in my front, and as we passed over his body he reached up his hand to the Captain and bade him goodbye.

After the first volleys we advanced loading and firing as rapidly as possible, and as we advanced, the enemy gave away before us. We soon reached the summit of the rise of ground before us, and passed over, sweeping the enemy before us until all had gone from sight, or sulked behind the fallen timber, or in the deep ravines. But as they were pressing hard on the 11th Illinois, we made a "right half wheel" and poured a murderous fire on the enemies flank for more than half an hour. The enemy finding their lines having given way in our front, opened again with grape and canister from their guns in the Fort, and we fell back to our original position, receiving the highest praise from our Colonel, as having done our work nobly.

Our loss thus far had been quite heavy. Our Color Sergeant, a noble young man, stood erect and bore the flag aloft until we reached the brow of the hill, when a ball struck him, and he fell mortally wounded, and the flag fell to the ground. In his dying agony he did not forget the flag, but pointed to it on the ground with the words, "See!! See!! See!!" We all understood what the poor fellow meant, and Conrad Scheffer dropped his gun, sprang to the flag, and bore it aloft during the rest of the battle. Private DeWitt Higgins was ordered off duty by the Surgeon on account of sickness, but when the battle opened, he sprang from the Ambulance, seized a gun and rushing to the front, fought like a tiger for an hour, but was killed.

At about 2 o'clock our Brigade was withdrawn to the rear to recuperate and give place to fresh troops. We moved by the left flank back on the ridge road and rested just out of reach of the enemies guns; but before the gap was filled, the foe perceiving our withdrawal, came rushing out with a great shout and fell heavily on the right flank of the remaining line, and the battle at this point became fearful. But the 23rd Ind. being fresh, were hastened forward attacking the "rebs" in the rear soon caused them to fall back to safer quarters behind their breast works.

While we were huddled together in the rear an aide-de-camp rode up from another part of the field and reported that General Smith had carried two lines of breastworks and was working his way into the Fort. He then proposed three cheers for the Union, which met with but feeble response, as most of the boys did not believe him, and as for our part of the field, we had really gained nothing, but had lost heavily in killed and wounded.

By 4 o'clock orders came from General Grant to press the battle to the utmost. So under cover of a ravine, our division was massed six columns deep for a last grand assault on the enemies works. To me this looked like rushing into the jaws of certain death. Their works were decidedly strong. The abbettis would give them time to shoot most of us down while we were working our way through it. Besides a third of our men had been killed, wounded or missing, and 'twas no wonder that Colonel Marsh exclaimed, "Is that all that's left of my Regiment?" But go we must. 'Twas ours to obey not plan, so our boxes were hastily filled, our guns made ready, but the order did not come to move forward; darkness was beginning to set in. The roar of musketry was gradually dying away, so withdrawing a little farther to the rear, we squatted on the ground, posted Sentinel, built fires, and prepared to spend the night.

And <u>such</u> a night! I shall never forget. Famished and chilled we huddled around our fires to doze, to freeze on one side, to burn on the other; while the wind sent puffs of smoke and ashes into our powder burnt faces. Thus we writhed and twisted on that damp cold ground, all that <u>gloomy night</u>. Around for miles lay our dead. The wounded - what could be found - had been collected and cared for by the Ambulance Corps.

We had no words of encouragement one for another. In fact, little was said. But it was the general feeling that the battle had gone badly. We had gained nothing but lost heavily, and they were still secure behind their breastworks, having a decided advantage over us, and we saw no hope for tomorrow but a repetition of today, and the prospect looked dark as the night that enshrouded us. Some stray shooting was done by the pickets during the night, but as we had become so accustomed to this, we paid no attention to it. The boys were truly exhausted, discouraged, disheartened; and oh, what would one give in a time like this, "a good square meal," and a warm bed where he may lay down in peace.

THE SURRENDER

Nearly dawn, we were enabled to obtain a kettle of hot coffee which together with some "hardtack" seemed to put a little better spirits into the boys. Soon "reveille" was sounded, we "fell in" for roll call, when the missing were noted. Then Colonel Marsh mounted his horse and the Regiment was formed. At the same time a courier clashed past saying <u>they had surrendered</u>. He rode with such lightening speed we could not get another word, but we did not believe him; however, Marsh ordered the Regiment forward saying, "Look well to your arms, it <u>may</u> be only a ruse to draw us on."

We moved cautiously until within sight of their parapets, when we could see white flags had been raised on every commanding position, and no hostile foe appeared to dispute our entrance inside the enclosure. It was now to us a certainty that the stronghold had surrendered with 16,000 prisoners, and a thrill of joy went through every loyal heart. As we passed down towards the fort proper, we passed long rows of log barracks in front of which the "Rebs" stood with their arms at their feet as docile as a wounded hart, and gazed intently on the hated Yankees as they filed past.

Captain Frisbie strutted proudly at the head of our company. I could see, as I gazed down the line in imagination, a score of feathers springing out the top of his slouch hat, and his feet flew up as lively as though he was stepping on something hot. His voice which was naturally squeaky, now rose to the highest pitch known to the musical scale, and louder than the screech of a steam tug's whistle, as he belched forth some word of command to all the conquering "Putnam Guards." Napoleon as he left Marengo could not have been more lifted up.

Our Brigade were the first troops to reach the main fort, when Captain Taylor rushed his battery in and fired a salute from the embrasure. Officers shook each other, and even embraced each other, and the crowd went wild with delight. Soldiers threw up their hats, pulled off their coats and fell to whipping one another until their wind gave out, or their coats went to pieces. This was the first great victory of the war, and the greatest day of rejoicing I ever saw. When these manifestations had somewhat subsided, a detail was sent out to bury the dead, while the rest of us made a raid on the "reb" commissary, which we found to consist of a bountiful supply, flour, bacon, corn meal, molasses, etc., etc., to which we fell with a will, cooking and eating, and sleeping in the warm quarters the rebs had built for us, until ordered hence.

We rested at Donaldson until the 1st of March, when we again moved back to the Tennessee river where a fleet of transports were being collected to transport the troops farther south. The roads were muddy, and 'twas not until the night of the 5th we reached the river, when weary of my hard day's march I laid down with my blankets around me on the hurricane deck of a steamer and slept finely, but in the morning I found myself under three inches of snow.

UP THE TENNESSEE

On the 14th of March there had been collected 120 steamboats and with these well loaded with troops and stores, we again began the ascent of the river. The water was high and navigation good, and with the boat decks black with soldiers and colors flying, I thought I never saw so grand a sight as we rounded the different bends in the river.

The inhabitants along the route seemed wild with delight, especially the women who manifested their joy by waving to us as long as there was a boat in sight. After spending several days on the water we disembarked at Savannah, Tenn., a small town on the east bank of the river. Here our division went into camp, while the main portion went into camp six miles farther up at a place called Pittsburg Landing.

Savannah was considered a loyal town, at least it had to be with its streets and houses filled with real live Yankees. The inhabitants took kindly to the soldiers, throwing open their houses to the sick and doing all in their power to help them. Here a large military hospital was established and a large amount of stores collected. Six days later we moved up the river by transports, to the landing; and went into camp about one mile and a half from the river on the main Corinth road, where we found excellent camping ground.

The situation was excellently chosen as on this side the river was high table land about 50 feet above the river, reaching from Lick Creek on the South to Owl Creek on the North. The ground was slightly rolling - many brooks of pure water were found in the ravines; and there was just timber enough to make a good shade in summer, but was easily passable by troops.

At the landing there was no town, but a good place for steamboats to land and unload goods which were hauled to the small towns by mules. On the bluffs near by were two small log houses which were used as a sort of store houses, but on our arrival were converted into hospitals.

Our camps covered a large area of this high table land. Sherman's Division was thrown forward about two miles from the Landing near the Shiloh Church. Prentiss to his left held the advance line, and consequently was the most exposed to the attacks of the enemy. Our own Division (McClernerd's) was camped 3/4 of a mile to the rear of Sherman's left. Then came the divisions of Hurlburt, Smiths and Stuarts, while General L. Wallace was at Crumps Landing with a division six miles below.

We soon had the ground cleaned, springs opened, while the sutlers arrived in great numbers, and we could buy all sorts of things without going off the ground, and as the weather had now become warm and grass was becoming green and the leaves were starting out from the trees, we were beginning to have delightful times. The Landing was now like a great City, full of life and animation. From morning until night heavy laden wagons were passing up and down the different roads; camps were moving to and fro at drill; from shop to shop some would wander in quest of bargains while everywhere could be seen fascinating groups earnestly engaged in the fascinating "Keno."

We had now over 30,000 troops on the field, and new Regiments were constantly arriving. The plan was to remain here until Buell should arrive with the Army of the Cumberland now on its way from Nashville by land, when with the combined forces an attack was to be made on Corinth where the rebel army were concentrating. Our officers did not dream of an attack. The troops were allowed to camp as suited their convenience without regard to order, and gaps of half a mile were left between some of the Divisions.

On Friday, the 4th of April, we were startled by brisk firing in Sherman's front; the long rolls were sounded when we flew to our arms and were in line immediately and stood for half an hour in readiness to await developments; but as the firing soon ceased, we were allowed to go to our tents, vowing that it was not healthy for an enemy to come fooling around here. We soon learned, however, that 'twas only a dash of the enemies cavalry on a picket post who had carried off a Lieutenant and several men. This did not arouse any suspicion among our officers, for no attempt was made at concentration, but the lines were left in the same careless manner as before.

BATTLE OF SHILOH

The morning of the 6th of April opened beautiful. We were astir early, as Sunday was always inspection day and we had to have our arms, clothing and quarters in the best of order; and when accomplished stood waiting for the Sergeants oft repeated call "fall in" for general inspection. The sun was just beginning to send her rays down through the young leaves that were springing from the boughs of the tall oaks. As we stood there, making plans for the day, the sound of a distant cannon fell on every listening ear. "What's that?" says Sam Forbes. No one dared to answer, but looked intently one at another. Soon another and another echoed among the trees. The drummers flew to their drums and rattled off the "long roll" with all their might; by this time every man had his accouterments on and was in ranks before our brass band had time to play one strain of "Hail Columbia."

By the time the Regiment was formed the shells came crashing through the trees into our camp. Then we could hear the rattle of musketry in front of Sherman. The ball had surely opened. Orderlies began to gallop from Regiment to Regiment with lightning speed. Officers hastily mounted their steeds, and hastily formed companies into regiments, and regiments into brigades.

Colonel Marsh was now in command of our brigade and we moved out of camp on the "double quick" with Lt. Col. Richards in command of the 20th Regiment. We moved in solid column "right in front" through the timber south to Sherman's support. It had not been more than ten minutes from the time of the first alarm before we were half a mile from camp, when we met a stream of wounded men coming back and many stragglers who had run without firing a shot.

We deployed in line to the left of Sherman on open ground sloping towards Lick Creek with Waterton's Battery on our right and Swartz's Battery left. In front of us we could see large masses of men filing into line, but as the sun was shining and the green leaves were coming out on the trees, gave their uniforms the appearance of blue instead of gray, and we dare not fire on them for fear they were our men. So Major Barletson rode down in advance but soon came galloping back with his arm shot off, shouting, "rebels! rebels!" At this our whole line opened fire, to which the enemy replied with spirit, and poured into us a murderous fire. We could not see them as they crouched down behind a rise of ground, while we were entirely exposed and within easy range of their guns. However, we gave them the best we had for half an hour, but their fire was telling fearful on our ranks, so much so, we had to load on our backs and fire on our knees to keep from all being killed, so our fire was not so rapid. Besides this, Waterhouse Battery gave away and abandoned all but one gun, when the enemy rushed forward with a yell and we had to fly from our position to a safer one in the rear. In falling back, we passed a line which had been formed a few rods in our rear, which opened fire as soon as we passed, thus holding the enemy temporarily in check. We halted our colors in rear of this line and tried to rally the scattered companies again for another stand, but of no avail, as the boys could not be formed under so severe a fire, and the ____ [this word not decipherable in Ira Blanchard's work] was not stayed until we reached our camps. Colonel Marsh rode along and severely reprimanded the officer for not making another stand before falling back so far, saying, "this battle would never be won with such fighting." As we halted on our camp ground to collect the men and reform, we had a good opportunity to look back on the conflict which was now raging less than a quarter of a mile from us. The roar and flash of the Artillery, the dashing hither and thither of horses, whose riders had been shot, the bursting of shell, the loud words of command, the screech of men as arms or legs would be shot off - all combined to make a picture that language fails to describe. Men who flew from the conflict through fear would almost invariably say "we're whipped, we're all cut to pieces," while those who had fought like men, but had to fall back on account of wounds, would report the fight as going splendid. An old dutchman from Swartz's Battery came flying back swinging his arms in the wildest manner, shouting at the top of his voice "Battery Swartz spiked mit mid wh-u-u-u."

The battle by this time had become general; all the troops were now engaged. The "rebs" were making a determined fight; the roar of battle could be heard for miles, extending from the Shiloh church back near the river. Sherman's men had been forced back to a new position near where our camps were, and General Prentiss had retreated with his shattered battalions, back to an old washed out road in which his men found shelter by lying down, and in this position they were enabled to resist the fierce charges of the enemy until late in the afternoon. Hurlburt was also being hard pressed, and his left had swung round quite a distance towards the Landing.

By eleven o'clock, our Brigade, now collected and supplied with ammunition, and being re-enforced by large details who had been out on guard, was again called into action. This time we deployed further to the left, across the upper Corinth road. The rebels had forced our lines back nearly a mile, and on our part of the field, the fighting was over the camps we occupied in the morning. We moved cautiously towards the enemy through the scattered timber, ducking our heads to escape the storm of grape and canister which was flying through the air, each man having his gun cocked and ready for the enemy wherever met. We halted in a ravine, where we were comparatively well protected by its steep sides, and at the same time we would have a good sweep of the ground beyond. What a splendid place to have faced the enemy we thought, but the enemy was too far off, and our men were holding them back and needed our help. Rising from the ravine we passed over a rise of ground and came in full view of the conflict. There was already a line of our men in front of us, bravely battling with the enemy and holding him in check; who as we approached made signs to us not to fire or mistake them for the enemy. We soon passed to the front of them and delivered our fire into the enemy's ranks with telling effect. Here we fought desperately, and the fierce charge of the enemy could not shake our solid ranks in the least; but in front of us we could see caissons exploding, horses dashing off without riders, and a general demoralization in their ranks. They had found a "hornets nest" and were getting stung. I think if we had made a charge then, we would have swept that part of the field. Colonel Richards walked up and down the line during this fierce conflict brandishing his navy revolver saying, "stand up to it boys, I'll shoot the first man that falters." The fighting here lasted two hours or more. Our guns became hot from constant firing. Ammunition had to be brought up from the rear. The ground was covered with the dead and dying. Wagons were smashed by exploding shell, and knapsacks, boxes and guns strew the ground. 'Twas a horrid sight. 'Twas here, as I was loading my gun for about the fiftieth time, I was struck by a musket ball, which entered the left arm at the elbow and slid up the bone about six inches, rendering the arm numb and useless. As I could not handle a gun with one hand I made my way to the rear, sought out a surgeon, had the large ounce ball extracted, the wound bandaged and my arm placed in a sling. The wound was painful, but I was still able to walk around and use my right arm. I thought at first to go back to the field and try and assist some of the wounded, but meeting John Henderson a member of our Company, crawling back, badly wounded, I helped him as best I could, back to the landing. Here we were taken on board a hospital ship, and kindly cared for by the nurses, most of whom were women. From the boat I could look out on the bluffs near the landing, where thousands were collected who had skulked away from their regiments and were crouching behind trees and rocks in abject terror, while men were entreating and threatening with every means in their power to induce them again to join their ranks and not disgrace their country, their flag. But all to no purpose; they clung to the shelter of the bluff as to dear life, and the crowd of panic stricken wretches kept increasing until the banks were black with them. Many tried to get on board the boats, but a man at each plank with drawn revolver prevented this. At one time the balls of the enemy began to fall in the water and the steamboat men began to be alarmed and shoved out from the shore, but they were soon ordered back. As they hauled in their planks I could see men clinging to spars and ropes; others swam panic stricken out into the stream and were drowned. If the sight along the line of battle was terrible, this along the landing was simply <u>horrible</u>. The wounded who could not walk were being brought back to the rear by hundreds, and at the old log house on the bluff, the saws and knives were cutting and sawing at human limbs and piling them in great heaps just outside, so that one would think he was near a butcher shop when trade was good. As I lay on the upper deck of that steamer, I kept my eyes intently fixed on the bluffs and expected every moment to see the white flag raised, and that devoted army surrender to the rebel horde that was pressing hard upon them at all points. Nearer and nearer came the rattle of musketry, and larger grew the crowd on the bluffs. As a last resort - as I thought - the Tyler and Conistoga which were near, opened fire and threw their 64lb. shell right up over the heads of our men in hopes they would fall in the enemies lines with telling effect.

Amid these scenes of gloom and uncertainty, a signal flag was waved from the bluff, when all eyes were turned to the opposite side of the river, and there to our great joy we beheld the advance of General Nelson's division of Buell's Army looking eagerly across. Our steamer though crowded with the wounded, was the first to go to ferry them across. We crowded together as best we could, and filled the decks with fresh troops, who, though having marched all day, seemed eager to get across and join the fray. We carried several loads over; the other boats did the same and soon this new addition were moving up the bluff and taking their places in front of the enemy, and we felt secure. By this time darkness had set in, rain came on, and the roar of battle had died away, and we could hear nothing but the moans of the wounded and dying, who were scattered for miles through the timbers, except when the gunboats sent their huge shell crashing amid the tall trees. We lay at the landing during the night, and early the next day were taken down to Savannah, and were quartered in stores, barns, or wherever we could find shelter.

Two days later I again visited that bloody field. Our men were in camp the same as before. The dead had all been buried, but a great deal of amputation was being done by the surgeons down at the old cabin by the landing. The tent which I formerly occupied remained intact. The Rebs had occupied it the night before, and probably left in a hurry, as they left some keepsakes which had been presented them by their friends at home when they went to war. We counted 128 bullet holes through the tent. In a clearing of about 120 acres, I counted 80 dead horses, and wagons, caissons, guns everywhere strew the ground, and the trees were torn and broken down by the heavy shot. The sight was truly sickening. I remained in hospital at Savannah about a week, and on receiving a twenty days furlough, started with my friend Neals Olsen (who was wounded about as I) for Illinois, and had quite an enjoyable time with my friends while nursing my wounded arm.

We returned early in May and reached Corinth the day after the rebels had evacuated that place and stayed over night within their old encampment near a house our surgeons were occupying, to care for the wounded who were being brought back from the pursuit of the rebel army. We looked the situation over carefully the next day, saw how our forces had moved cautiously up from the old battle ground a distance of twenty-two miles, the different lines they had fortified, how near they had come at last of surrounding and probably capturing that vast army, which had wisely skipped out during the night, leaving large quantities of stores behind.

The next day we sought out our regiment and reported for duty. But now as the Rebs had gone there was now no longer need of so large an army here. So the army under Grant was sent to different points along the Memphis and Charleston Railroad, or moved to places where there was the most need.

JACKSON, TENNESSEE

Colonel Marsh was ordered to move with his Brigade west and occupy Jackson, a large town on the Columbus and New Orleans Railroad, which we reached after two days march. We entered the town on

Sunday about noon, which we found to be a fine wealthy town, but terribly bitter against the "northern hordes."

Secession was rank. The place had furnished a full regiment for the Confederate Army, and we could see nothing but malice depicted on every countenance. We stacked our arms in the street and lounged idly on the walks while our camping grounds were being selected. Our faces were now covered with dust down through which the lines of perspiration ran until 'twould have been hard to tell to what race or nationality we belonged. The ladies gathered up their skirts, turned up their noses and skipped away with the utmost horror at sight of the animals; but the darkies as they came out of their church that day, took in the sight more composedly, and would even venture to touch a gun with the tip of their gloved fingers, and hang around as though 'twas a sight not often seen, and one old negress was actually heard to exclaim, "De Lor bless you all" and 'twas long before the crowd of dusky worshipers moved away. Our camp was in a beautiful grove on the main street of the town. Soon we had our oven built, and we were supplied with fine soft bread, fresh beef arrived, and we soon began to live like Lords. The next Sunday we attended the Methodist Church, the soldiers occupying two thirds of the seats, which seemed to be quite a surprise to the regular church goers. The ladies would no more come near us than they would a snake, although we were now brushed up and looked quite respectable. The preacher seemed quite a talented man, but we soon learned from his tone and manner that he was a rank secesh; however, we kept on going, and soon crowded his former flock out and Mister Preacher skipped the town and we put our own Chaplain in charge.

In the afternoon came the colored worshipers in the same church, but in the basement. They had no preacher, but the meeting was presided over by one of the white "brudren" which we also attended, more out of curiosity than anything else. The meeting was well attended, full to overflowing, so some of us had to look in at the windows, which we always preferred, as the odor of such a congregation was not particularly agreeable on a warm day. The costumes was the most interesting part of the programme to us. Men who had toiled all the week with bare head and back in the cotton fields, under a broiling sun, would come to church on Sunday in the finest broadcloth, stove pipe hat, white kid gloves carrying a huge umbrella that a ray of the sun might not penetrate to his black hide. The women, the young ones especially, their gaudy costumes could hardly be described. The nips, the swings the flirts as they tripped daintily along with fan and parasol grinning and showing "de white ob de eye" to whoever they met.

At the opening hymn we almost thought we were caught up into the third heavens, such a swell of melody came from a hundred voices as they chanted

> "Bredren dear dont get a weary
> Bredren dear dont get a weary
> Bredren dear dont get a weary
> Your work be almost done."

Then came the still more inspiring one of "I'm guine away to glory hallaluyah" but before it was finished many of the dusky sisters had risen to their feet and were clapping their hands shouting "glora" and one more earnest than the rest would jump up full two feet from the floor every time they came to the "hallaluyah." Thus the racket was kept up for half an hour, singing, shouting, jumping and clapping of hands. The white "bruder" tried to get in a few words of exhortation but 'twas of little use, for the singing had started the old flame and all went shouting on their way to Glory-ah.

The Railroad was soon repaired back to Columbus and trains began to arrive with stores from the North. As soon as trains could be run, Colonel Marsh, Commander of the Post, issued a proclamation that all male citizens over sixteen years of age, should come to the Courthouse and register and take the oath of allegiance within five days, or be transported North as prisoners of war. But before the five days had expired many of the most prominent had skipped during the night, among whom was our Methodist preacher. So we resolved ourselves into a conference and appointed one of our own number to preach, and had things our own way after that.

BLACK BEN

A boy, about twelve years old, used to bring to our camp, daily, a basket with fresh butter, eggs, etc., from his old "missus," to sell to the boys in camp, as the white people soon found the soldiers good customers for such things. Ben was a fine black boy; everybody liked him. His head was like the swab of a cannon; a perfect mat of wool, with lips thick as a calf's liver, and when he grinned displayed the most perfect set of ivories, that ever adorned the mouth of a nigger.

There was only one fault with Ben; when he got asleep he was stiff as a poker and 'twas next to impossible to wake him up. We used to roll him down hill, stand his stiff carcass up against a tree or put live coals to his feet before we could make him budge. However the boys liked Ben and Ben liked the boys. So Ben thought he'd run away. So one dark night one of our picket posts was startled on seeing a dark object approach them. "Halt! who goes there?" cries the sentinel. At this every man seizes his gun and stands ready. "It's me," says the dark object, "what toats you all dem butter and eggs every day for old missus don ye know me? I's Ben."

"Advance Ben, and give the countersign!" came again from the sentinel.

"Hant got no coun'sn."

"Halt!" says the sentinel, "what's that you've got in your hand?"

"Dats de Banjo I bought wid me own money and had to be mighty suple to git off wid dat; an massa Yankee if y'll let me go wid ye, I'll gib ye dat." So the boys took Ben and his old banjo into camp attached him to our Company as cook, which he soon learned to perfection. He also learned to read, and became the most faithful boy I ever saw; and long into the night when all work was o'er, Ben could be seen sitting on a log or stump, picking at his old banjo, and humming some of the sweetest melodies. He followed us during the war sharing our trials and privations, always ready to lend a helping to those in distress and would often face dangers that the bravest would often shun. In fact he became the favorite of the Company, so much so, that he was taken North at the close of the war and placed on a farm.

We spent the greater part of the summer of '62 in and about Jackson. The citizens, those who remained, soon found the hated Yankees their best friends. Trade everywhere revived and money plenty; money too they were glad to get in preference to their own worthless Confederate Script which was almost worthless. 'Tis true the streets were constantly patrolled by soldiers and martial law was rigidly enforced; yet large amounts of cotton were purchased by Northern speculators at enormous prices; and private property was respected and even guarded, and the poor were in many cases fed from our Commissary.

ALEX. McPHERSON

We of course passed a pleasant time during our sojourn here. The Forked Deer ran within half a mile of town, down which we used to wander on fishing excursions, or to gather the sweet mulberries which grew in abundance along its banks.

One cloudy day Russell Gowdy, Joe Getold, Alex McPherson and myself wandered a long way down this stream in quest of fish, and in returning tried to shorten the distance by passing through Cane Brake, but as we could not see the sun and had nothing to guide us, we soon lost our way and wandered around in a circle most of the day. It was extremely laborious working our way through the thick canes, and we became greatly exhausted, and I noticed that Alex every time we found we were going wrong and would change our course, would burst out in an unusual fit of laughter as he followed on. We reached camp however before dark, but poor Alex continued his fits of laughter and in a few days he became violently insane, when he was sent home, and the last we heard of him he had drowned himself in the Illinois river near La Salle.

CAMP ON THE HATCHEE

About the first of August the 31st and 20th Regiments were sent with a section of Waterhouse Battery, to hold the ford across the Hatchee about 40 miles distance from Jackson. After a hard march of two days, we arrived at the ford after dark, threw out sentinels and went to sleep in the timber. About 12 o'clock I was awakened by Johnny Rurdon, a little Englishman of our Company shaking me and saying, "Blanch, wake up; see what a nice nigger I've brought you." Johnny had been out on some of the neighboring plantations - I requested Johnny to leave me alone; let the darkey lie down until morning and I'd see what the animal looked like. In the morn Sambo was on hand, a fine specimen of the patent-leather skinned tribe of humanity which Johnny said he had "jerked" from a plantation about a mile distant. I put him at work taking care of my gun, knapsack, canteen and haversack, and made him quite useful for about two weeks; but when the first fighting began Mr. Nigger, traps and all, were gone.

After resting a few days the boys sought the neighboring plantation in quest of plunder, as the country round about was extremely rich in all that was calculated to tickle the appetite of a soldier, and many's the load of chickens, turkeys and sheep that found their way to our commissary. Fruit was beginning to get ripe, and there was no day that there was not an abundant supply in our camp.

We found a Cider Mill on a plantation and set the darkies at work making cider for the crowd. Our camp was constantly thronged with negroes, who wanted to go along with us, but those we did not need were driven away. One old darkie I remember by the name of Klem came with the plea that we ought to take him, for he could steal better than any nigger in the neighborhood. We tried him, let him sleep during the day, and at night he would strike out, and never failed to come back in the morning loaded down with calves, sheep, chickens or whatever he could lay his hands on.

One young buck - in handling a gun - a thing they were not allowed to do - accidently shot another negro wounding him severely in the face. We tied him to a tree, binding his hands together back of him on the opposite side of the tree, telling him he had better make his peace with God as he would be shot at noon. The poor fellow was wild with fright. He writhed in mortal agony for more than an hour; he groaned, prayed and begged for mercy at the hands of a just God, saying he deserved no mercy at the hands of his white "bredren" he had committed a great crime and deserved to die, "But, O-o-o- wuld de gu Lor up in glory hab mercy on a por nigger's soul."   His face underwent the most fearful contortions.   His eyes protruded from their sockets, as the time of execution drew nigh.   Had he not been lashed to a tree, his trembling limbs could not have sustained him.   I never looked upon a picture of such utter despair.

When we considered him sufficiently punished we let him go; and I venture to say he was never seen around the camps of the Yankees again.

I confess it was with regret that we struck tents at this point again to move back to Jackson which had now become quite an important military post of western Tennessee.   The railroads had now been repaired through this part of the State and west to Memphis and were guarded by bands of soldiers at each town who threw their sentinels far out along the tracks in either direction, thus rendering transportation of stores comparatively safe.

We had not traveled far in the direction of Jackson when we were met by a courier with orders to change our course to the South, and go to the relief of the garrison at a place called Meden on the Columbus and New Orleans Railroad.

BATTLE OF BRITTONS LANE

As we were moving rapidly forward, our advance guard by some mistake led us off the main road, by a shorter cut through the timber called "Brittons Lane."   Before we were half way through this lane we were startled by the sharp crack of two or three guns in our front.

Colonel Shred of the 31st who was in command, hastily sent forward to ascertain what the matter was.   Soon the aide rode back and reported cavalry, when the two guns were hastened forward to shell them, but their advance fell back across an open field through which the main road ran.

Our two regiments formed in front of this open field on either side of the road; the two guns to our left and a squad of cavalry to our right, in all not over 1500 men, as many from each Regiment were on detached duty.

We had no sooner formed our line than the enemy sent up a hideous yell from the timber on the opposite side of the field. We knew by this they meant business, and that soon there would be "music in the air." Everything was hastily made ready. Boxes open, bayonets set, now as, Shakespeare would say, "Then set the teeth, and stretch the nostrils wide" and prepared for the inevitable. We had not long to wait. Soon from out the timber poured the host. Line upon line they came, with sabers lifted high in air at full gallop. The very ground trembled beneath their tread. We were astonished at their numbers, yet our little band stood firm as though transfixed to the ground on which they stood.

"Let them come; let them come!" shouted some stout heart. They did come, to meet a sheet of flame and a shower of lead from the muzzles of our muskets. The two cannon had been loaded with canister and made a fearful havoc in their ranks. Many a brave one fell from his horse; which went dashing away.

At this first volley they were thrown into confusion, but they soon rally and come on again, and we give them the best we have. Again and again they charge, and fight desperately. They ride close up to our ranks and one more daring than the rest, dismounts and tries to cut his way through our ranks with his sword, but was shot down by Ashley of our Company. We hold our ground nobly while they make several desperate charges, and the field in front of us is now strewn with horses and men. Now a force comes pouring down on our left flank and charge upon our guns at the same time throwing a force upon our flank which divided our fire, and after a desperate struggle the guns fell into their hands.

Our force was by this time becoming considerably scattered; and things began to look rather gloomy when finding we were being surrounded, fell back a little into the timber. Here we formed a hollow square, and repulsed every attempt to break it. Finally they withdraw leaving 65 of their dead on the field and the hated Yankees masters of the situation, having captured their colors and quite an amount of small arms. Our loss was only 4 killed and 40 wounded. This was considered the most brilliant affair of the war thus far, and the Jackson paper the next day published an extra loudly extolling the boys of the 31st and 20th regiments 1500 strong for meeting and defeating Billy Jackson's Cavalry 8000 strong. We buried our dead and cared for the wounded and remained on the field during the night and moved on to Meden the next day without opposition; spent a couple of days at that place, and again took up our line of march 'tords Jackson.

As we neared the city, we learned something of how the news had preceded us and was received by the inhabitants and every man braced himself up to enter town, as a conquering hero. Captain Frisbie as usual, "strutted and bellowed" at the head of the 20th. The "Secesh" flag was carried at the tail end of the line, and almost every man had some sword or gun taken from the "rebs." Colonel Shred, a modest unassuming man rode calmly at the head of the column as though nothing had happened, though one of his arms had been partly carried off by a ball and he had lost his hat in the engagement.

The bells were rung, and cannon fired as we moved up the street; and men, women and children filled the walks. What cheering! What shouting! everywhere greeted us. Then we were massed in the Court House square where General Logan spoke to the crowd eulogizing us as the most undaunted heroes of the nineteenth century.

ZELA

Soon after our entry into the City of Jackson a young slave girl who had been tenderly reared for questionable purposes, by a young planter, becoming dissatisfied with her master, sought a refuge among the newly arrived Yankees. Her tender years and great beauty of face and figure made her an object of pity as well as of attraction, and she found no difficulty in enlisting the sympathies of men and officers who freely gave her money and promised to protect her from the cruelty and lust of her former master. She was employed at the Court House by the Provost Marshall, as laundress and prospered finely financially and in all the graces that contribute to the adornment of lovely young womanhood. She seemed much attached to the Yankees, and rejoiced that she was at last free and away from the contaminating influences of her master. She remained with us about two months, during which time she had improved greatly but all this time the jealous wrath of her master knew no bounds. The green-eyed monster had completely taken possession of his soul. To think that those "Blue-Bellied Yankees" should have his beautiful Mulatto girl, his charming Zela; she who would bring a $1000. in any market; the thought was unendurable and by the Gods of war he'd have her back! Many plans were laid; but the girl was too well protected. All failed. He dare not go in person and force her away. The "Yanks" would lock him up in the jail close by; finally he bribed another girl to go to her room and say her master was very sick and could not live but a few hours; and before his death he desired to see his dear little Zela once again. Zela thought if he was so near deaths door, she might with safety go, yea she ought to go and see the one that had brought her up from a child, and cared for her all her life. Not doubting but that the story was true, for 'twas told by one of her friends, she put on her hat and went timidly 'tords her master's house. The door no sooner closed behind her, than her master, who was lying on a sofa, sprang to his feet, seized her by the throat and saying with a great oath_____ I've got you now_____ [Here was evidently an omitted profanity.] Her hands were bound, a gag put in her mouth, and she was taken in a buggy outside the lines by a sly route and driven to Holly Springs where she was sold to a Planter of Georgia where she was put at work in the field until Lincoln's Proclamation again made her free, when she married, came North, and she now resides in Chicago and is the mother of several little woolly heads.

Again we were sent out a Railroad guard. This time twenty miles north; and were camped on the plantation of Colonel Harris, where foraging was extremely rich, and as usual we employed old Klem to do the night work, and we fared well each day. On this plantation there were 180 slaves who went out at break of day, at the blast of the driver's horn and toiled in the cotton fields until the shade of night; each carrying by way of lunch a corn "Pone" and a bottle of sour milk. There was no great traffic in slaves in those days; slave property was not a good investment during the war, yet those who owned them held on to them as tenaciously as ever.

We had a man in our regiment, a bold bad man, who would dress up in citizen's clothes, take a young darky three or four miles away from camp, sell him for what he could get, saying he was going into the Confederate Army, then in a few hours he would steal him back again and sell him the second, third and some times the fourth time in one day. As we stayed near the plantation, the slaves became more and more independent, and the drivers were gradually losing control over them. Our Chaplain would preach to large crowds of them on Sundays as they hung around camp, but he always exhorted them to remain quietly at home and obey their masters and see what the hand of the Lord would do for them by way of their deliverance from slavery; but they constantly crowded our camps always desiring to go along with the Yankees.

Our Captain Frisbie had now been promoted to Major of the Regiment by reason of gallant conduct at Brittons Lane, and Lt. Vic. Stevens was in command of our Co. H. We remained at the plantation until the weather began to get cooler and troops could be moved with less danger from heat; besides there was a vast deal of marching and fighting to do before the great rebellion would be crushed.

PART III

On The Move Again

RAID ON THE SUTLER

On the 10th of November we were ordered back to Jackson where troops were being collected preparatory to a move farther south. We arrived in town about 10 o'clock p.m., but as we intended to move on the next day, did not pitch our tents, but built some fires rolled ourselves up in our blankets and lay down on the ground near the railroad for the night. I could not sleep very well, for some of the boys were constantly going and coming and whispering among themselves, but I had no idea that mischief was going on until near morning, when I was awakened by the sound of cracking of nuts, opening bottles, breaking cans, etc., and I soon learned the feasting was going on at a great rate around the fires. Even then I had no idea of the extent of the mischief that was being done. A portion of the regiment had broken open the post Sutler's tent, where several thousand dollars worth of goods were stored, and loaded on to the train which was to take us south the next day, most of the plunder which they concealed under the baggage. Frisbie knowing the boys had been in mischief, stayed behind a day as the train moved on, leaving Jack Tunison in command but made no effort to prevent the goods from being carried off; and even at the first halt, when the regiment was ordered searched, the officers slyly passed word around telling the boys to bury what they had so they could not be found. The search was made at a small town some fifty miles from Jackson and resulted in finding nothing. Nevertheless, when the facts were laid

before Grant, he promptly assessed the regiments the full amount of
damages and dismissed Frisbie and Tunison from the service and sent
them home in disgrace.

LA GRANGE

We arrived at this place on the 10th of November [date may be in error
as Blanchard uses the same date in RAID ON THE SUTLER]. This is
quite a railroad center and troops are arriving from all quarters
preparatory to a grand move down along the New Orleans road to
operate against Vicksburg.

La Grange is a fine wealthy town having many splendid buildings, but
the people thoroughly given over to the Southern cause. On our arrival
most of the inhabitants left taking all movable property with them.

We covered the fields around the town with our tents, and the camp
fires smoked for miles around, lighting up the sky like the lamps of a
great city, and the roll of drums at "tatoo" and "reveille" sounded far and
near calling companies to ranks for roll call. Many of the officers
quartered in some of the most elegant private residences. Colonel
Marsh especially secured the finest and hung out a monster flag as a
signal for Brigade Headquarters. 'Twas here the troops were reviewed
by our new Corps Commander, Major General McPherson. Here our
songs of glee could be heard in our tents at night, as the spirit of song
had taken hold of the boys wonderfully, and here we listened to many
exhortations from our good Chaplain Button, who would take a barrel
or stump for a pulpit and sing out, "Oh yes! Oh yes! Run here
everybody. We're going to sing you a temperance song and tell you
something about the war." If this did not bring the crowd, he would get
some one to sing, "All hail the power of Jesus name" or "How tedious
and tasteless the hour" when heads would peep out of the tents as if to
inquire what was the matter? Then the crowd would begin to gather.
Some without coat or boots, some bringing their blankets and would
stretch themselves out at full length on the ground, and if the sermon
was not particularly interesting, would gradually slip away, one by one,

and often the poor man would be left to finish his sermon alone. When Captain Bradley was sent from headquarters to take command of the Regiment - he having been detailed on the General's Staff - in place of Frisbie who was removed, the boys rose in open rebellion and "Whiskey Dan" was shouted after him wherever he went. "I <u>will</u> maintain discipline in the Regiment in spite of fate," shouted Dan in a speech to the boys soon after assuming command; "and if you don't behave I'll put you all under <u>arrest</u>." But "Whiskey Dan" soon won the respect of the boys and things went on as smoothly as ever. But the boys always maintained that Dan was the best judge of whiskey there was in the regiment.

About the first of December we were again in motion, following South along the Railroad which was put in repairs by companies of Sappers and Miners that supplies for this vast army might be brought forward promptly. The roads by this time had become muddy, and our progress was necessarily slow, besides the enemies cavalry constantly harassed our vanguard, but at all points were driven like chaff before the wind. The people along the road displayed the white flag from their houses in token of submission, but if a soldier should approach a dwelling the women would almost invariably cry from the windows, "Smallpox here, dare you come in?" But we soon caught on to the dodge and if they said Smallpox would reply, "Oh yes, that's what were looking for." And if they had any hams in the smokehouse, or any chickens, they were very apt to suffer.

Thus we went on day after day through forests, over hill and across streams, at times drenched with rain, and again suffering for water, mostly through a wild and desolate country until we reached

HOLLY SPRINGS,

a beautiful town of Northern Mississippi, where we were allowed to rest awhile, until the road was repaired and stores collected; then again after filling our wagons and haversacks afresh, we again pushed on through the mud and rain. As we advanced farther 'tords the south the enemies forces were constantly augmented and resistance became more obstinate, and infantry and light artillery was used at many points to dispute our progress. At the Yazoo they had erected fortifications but abandoned them on our approach and we pushed rapidly on after the flying "rebs" and took about 1200 prisoners.

We were now in better country and much better roads and the weather warm and pleasant. From this on it was a running fight with the flying "rebs." They made no other stand but took to the woods and swamps, each man for himself, and our cavalry gobbled most of them.

OXFORD

we reached on the tenth of January and filled the Courthouse to overflowing with our prisoners. Oxford is an important town of about 5000 inhabitants; is the seat of the State University and the residence of some of the most prominent men of the State.

Our regiment went into camp in the Courthouse square, hence it devolved on us to guard the prisoners, which were a motley crowd, having all sorts of uniforms, from the commonest homespun deeply dyed in dirt to the more stylish Kentucky Jeans of a rich butternut hue. They were of all nationalities and ages. Boys and old men, spindle shanks and the fat fussy Dutchman. But their greatest peculiarity was their constant cry for something to eat. They acted as though they had not had anything to eat for a month. They were fed three times a day from our Commissary, yet they were begging from morning until night for more, and would let down strings from the upper windows and beg the boys to tie on crackers, bacon, or whatever they could eat.

On our arrival in town many of the boys as usual pillaged the town, and coming across a cellar well stored with wine, it was not long before half the regiment was staving drunk and music filled the air for a time.

I selected a store, facing on the square, for my quarters, to be nice and dry in case of rain. A jeweler who had followed the army for trade opened his wares in the front window, so we concluded we would chum together. In the rooms above were some chairs, a table, bedstead, but no clothing for the bed. So when night came on we started out to supply the articles needful for light housekeeping. We tried many a house before we found anything that we would carry off. At last when about a mile from town we came to a fine house, apparently deserted, but the doors securely barred. Getting a rail which we used as a battering ram we soon effected an entrance, and there to our joy, what a wealth of things needful were stored. We selected a fine large featherbed and tugged it back to town. When we had the thing safely deposited in our room a new and unforeseen difficulty presented itself. My friend being of German descent insisted on sleeping underneath this load of feathers, while I of keeping on top. Finally we concluded to sleep cross-wise, he at one end underneath while I at the other end on top.

We were at this place about three weeks pillaging the town and having a fine time generally, as we had appropriated most everything in the town to our own use. When about 12 o'clock one night the "long roll" was sounded and every man sprang to his arms. The enemy cavalry had made a dash on Holly Springs, our base of supplies, overpowered the guard under Colonel Marsh and burned all the stores which had been collected there, together with some of the railroad bridges across the streams.

This of course was a check to our farther progress southward along this line, as the country through which we passed was poor and could not subsist so vast an army a day. So with our supplies gone, there was nothing else to do but to retrace our steps, or starvation would soon be the consequence.

Again the army began to move; this time our colors pointed North, and after a number of weary days march through mud and rain we again crossed a tributary of the Yazoo and our brigade went into camp while the main army pushed on farther north to where communication was open and where subsistence could be obtained.

We lay on the Yazoo ten days during which time it rained continuous.

Why we were left here I never knew. No enemy seemed to trouble or threaten our rear. We would have starved here had not our cavalry brought in some corn in the ear which we parched and subsisted on during our stay, and with cold, wet and hunger our sufferings became intense.

All our search for hogs or cattle were in vain; there were none to be found in the country round about; and if we were lucky enough to find an old dame who would make up a cup of Sassafras tea, we considered ourselves fortunate. Yet as we were compelled by hunger, we kept on seeking through the wet and among a poor and beastly ignorant people. When out foraging one day, we reined up in front of a log cabin when the old woman came out and addressed us thus:

"Now what do you uns want ter come down her agin we uns for? We uns don't want u-uns around here. An 'twas a right smart o'chickens I missed when Captain Sherman comed round here with his critter Co. and tread down most my taters dare, and toted off a right smart o baken from my smoke house there."

I was sergeant of the guard once while in this lonely region, and 'twas my duty to travel from post to post unarmed and see that all was well. This should be done at stated intervals during the night. The posts were thrown out a long distance to guard against any surprise, and the night was extremely dark, and to travel through the dense forests alone in the night, when the bush-whackers were prowling around, when to find the way was difficult, was not so pleasant a task as one might suppose, when he is at home and comfortably sleeping in his bed. Nevertheless, I have traveled this lonely way many a night, some times half asleep, to be awakened by the sentinel's cry of, "Who goes there?" Then to advance and whisper the countersign over the point of the bayonet to the sentinel, who through the least mistake might shoot you down in your tracks.

On the night in question we were fearful the enemy was near, our guard was doubled and thrown farther out. I started at 10 o'clock to make the rounds; I lost my way several times; I crossed over streams, I waded through swamps, and only completed the circuit by break of day. But I think that night's experience was harder to me than a year of common toil. I fancied my hair had all turned gray during the night, at least it had stood much on end.

Leaving this dreary wilderness, we again moved north, and after a few days travel we found ourselves in a much better country, where cattle, sheep and hogs were abundant. As soon as our tents were pitched at night, scores of the boys would strike out with their guns and shoot whatever was eatable and soon the camp would be supplied with abundance of fresh meat. The officers would make some pretense of opposition to this wanton destruction of property but their efforts to prevent it were so feeble that the work went bravely on, yet occasionally one would get punished.

We had a man in our Company called Father Ashley. He never would steal; not he; he was too well brought up in old Vermont; he would even curse those who did and the officers that allowed it. But one night after a long day's march being tired and hungry, Father thought he'd strike out. A number of boys had passed out of camp with their guns, and if questioned by the Colonel would say they were going out to clean their guns or something of that sort. The Colonel spied Ashley as he was making off with his gun and calls, "Hello there! Where are you going?"

"I'm going to shoot a hog," says Ashley; he could not tell a lie. "Put down that gun," says the Colonel, "and carry this log for two hours." So poor Ashley was put under guard and compelled to march backwards and forth with a heavy log on his back long after the boys had returned with their plunder and were feasting and resting inside their tents. But when he did get off he was a sight to behold. The boys laughed, while he cursed the army, the officers, the country, the flag and mankind in general. But Father Ashley felt better after he had devoured a leg of mutton and taking an enormous chew of tobacco, but I always pitied the man who ever after that spoke to him about shooting a hog.

We continued our march now west along the state line stopping at some of the towns a day or two at a time and arrived at Memphis early in

January 1863, and went into camp in the suburbs of the city where we were soon well fixed and ready to enjoy the much needed rest which was promised us after our weary march for the last six weeks.

MEMPHIS

Here we enjoyed for a time many of the privileges of a great city. Having little to do, we frequently attended the churches, theaters and other places of amusement, when we could be spared from our regular duty, and passed much of the time during our sojourn here in pleasantness and peace.

On the 15th of January, two soldiers of Co. B., while strolling far out of the city among the rural population, called at a lonely house, as soldiers often do, and ordered a dinner cooked. All went well until they had finished their meal and were about to depart, when all at once three strangers put in an appearance and informed the soldiers they were prisoners. "All right," says one of the boys, "we did not intend to go back to the Yankee Camp. We slipped off last night with the intention of making our way north and we expect that soon they will be looking for us." Thus these two boys succeeded in persuading the "Rebs" that they were deserters and that there were hundreds in the Yankee camp who were ready to desert at the first opportunity, saying they would not serve longer if the object of the war was to free the negroes. This was just after the emancipation proclamation.

After a long parley 'twas finally agreed that the two soldiers should go back to camp after 'twas dark, and persuade as many boys to leave as possible, but only a few come at once; that they would be allowed to travel unmolested through the Confederacy until they reached their home, if they would swear never again to take up arms against the south.

The two boys were also promised $15 each for all the guns they could bring and be conducted to a safe retreat until all danger of pursuit was over and they were well on their way north. They also said they were agents of the Davis Gov. that they were sent to help those who were dissatisfied to desert and that they were supplied with money by their government for that very purpose.

The boys reached camp soon after dark and instead of trying to persuade any to desert, reported the facts to the officer of the day, who gave John McEowen and twenty of us permission to go in pursuit of the spies. We reached the cabin about 11 o'clock that night and came up to it from all sides with bayonets fixed; then the two boys were sent to rap on the door and inform them that we had come with our guns, which they saw on opening the door, all pointing at them. They had not another word to say; they found they were caught and submitted as meekly as lambs. We marched them back to camp, lodged them in jail and were highly commended by the Commanding General.

LAKE PROVIDENCE

On the first of February a large fleet was again called and we moved down the Mississippi as far as Lake Providence on the Louisiana side. The lake is about one mile wide and thirteen long, and its surface is about 15 ft. below the water of the Mississippi. Standing on the side of the lake you have to look up to see the boats as they pass down the river. Along the banks of the lake some beautiful specimens of Holly and Sycamore grow whose branches are hung with a white specimen of parasite moss, which looks from a distance like a sheet of falling water. The country around is low and level but exceedingly fertile and covered with some fine plantations. Along the shores the land was dry and sandy and made an excellent camping ground. At the head of the lake was a small town close up to the levee, which divided the waters of the lake from the river. Here our stores were placed for a time while the army were encamped for miles back along the south bank of the lake.

In a few days we had constructed a number of small boats in which we used to cross and recross this beautiful sheet of water in quest of plunder; and as the weather had now become warm we spent many a happy day in this one locality.

LITTLE LAURA

One day as friend Olsen and I were out for a stroll we spied at play not far from a cabin, a little girl about 5 years old. She was dressed in the most common of homespun cotton, which had never been colored, and without hat or shoes. Her white skin, long curly hair and beautiful face attracted our attention, for she was not like the other children in the neighborhood who, if you stopped to talk to them would come crowding around with "give me dis, give me dat" but she was modest and shy of strangers, and 'twas with some difficulty that we could talk to her at all. However, after we had parted with some pennies, we became fast friends and she soon began to like the soldiers much. She took me one day to see her "mudder" whom I found to be a fine lady, almost white, though a slave, and she had for a husband a man about as black as the blackest. She told me the father of Laura was the owner of the plantation, but was now an officer in the Southern Army, for whom she had been a slave for many years.

I used to go to the little girl's house almost daily, and found her to be the sweetest little child I ever met. To gain her confidence I always took her some little present that she might rejoice when the soldiers came, and many an hour I spent learning her to read, or telling her stories of what there was way up in the country where the soldiers came from.

CUTTING THE LEVEE

During our stay at the lake all sorts of experiments had been tried to find a way to run boats past the blockade at Vicksburg, but all had failed. As a last resort, by turning the water from the river into this lake, they hoped to secure a passage from the lake out through some of the byous into the Tensas. The troops break camp. The stores put on steamers, the steamers which were lying along the levee, then all the troops were taken on board, and all was in readiness, when a small channel was cut through the bank and the water began to pour through down into the lake. The little stream soon increased to a mighty torrent as the banks gave way.

Some sailors from one of the Gun Boats got out their life boat and jumping in went down over the cataract holding their oars high in the air. To add to the grandeur of the scene, some soldiers set fire to the buildings of the town, and for a time it was a grand panorama of fire and water doing their destructive work. The country around was soon flooded and the inhabitants, what were left, had to flee with their earthly effects for their lives to higher ground for safety but what became of little Laura, I never knew.

MILLIKIN'S BEND

is just above the mouth of the Yazoo river or the enemies batteries at Hains Bluff. The entire 17th Army Corps were encamped here in the very Garden of Eden. Everything was now green and the long lines of rose hedges were in full bloom. Other troops were in camp near by and all preparations were being made for a general advance on Vicksburg. In the two years which had elapsed since our enlistment, many changes had taken place in our ranks. Colonel Marsh resigned at Memphis and Colonel Richards was in command with Bradley second. The Surgeons Goodbrake and Baley had gone home and left a Dr. Richards in their place. Button our Chaplain had resigned and left a young preacher to attend to the spiritual wants of the boys, also by the name of Richards. The heads of Companies had most all changed. Our own Co. "H" was commanded by V. H. Stevens with John McEowen and William Ware as Lieutenants. Thomas Margrave was Orderly Sergeant. Sam Forbes, O. B. Champany, John Henderson, J. Cunningham and several others had been discharged on account of wounds. A number had been killed, others had contracted diseases and were discharged for disability, so that with all our recruits we did not muster more than seventy-five men. Yet those who remained were of the hardiest kind, being thoroughly schooled in the art of war, and seasoned to endure the greatest hardships. The officers too made fewer mistakes, and a move now was generally made in the right direction. Our many victories had given the men confidence in themselves, and when we faced an enemy, retreat was not thought of; but the motto now was "Conquer or die."

Yet, as I have hinted before, many vices had crept in. Gambling was carried on to an alarming extent in spite of the vigilance of the officers, and many a one after receiving his pay would not sleep until all was lost at "Keno" or "draw poker."   Stealing for the mere fun of the thing had become chronic, and helpless women and children suffered much abuse at the hands of the "hateful Yankees" as they called us. Private property was nowhere respected, and it is no wonder that the inhabitants of the South fled in abject terror at the approach of the "hordes of the North."

Governor Dick Yates paid us a visit at this place and spoke to our Brigade "en mass" on horseback. In his speech he alluded to the State of Louisiana as having been purchased by the general government at a cost of ten million dollars; and "by heaven" said he, "we will redeem it, or make it one vast burying-ground."

His speech caused great enthusiasm among the troops, and the Governor was loudly cheered; especially when he presented our own Twentieth Regiment with a beautiful silken flag.

RUNNING THE BLOCKADE

On the twentieth of April volunteers were called for, who were willing to take their lives in their hands and go with the fleet which was being made ready to make the hazardous attempt to run past the batteries of Vicksburg during the night. Forty good men were wanted and over two hundred volunteered. From our company was John Norris and John Henry Cassell who was on a boat that sank, when they swam ashore and were taken prisoners.

General Logan said to the boys before starting; "I want no faltering, if any man attempts to leave his post, I want him shot on the spot."

The fleet consisted of four iron-clad gun boats, two wooden ones and a dozen steamers and several barges heavily loaded with commissary stores and munitions of war for the army below. These were protected on all sides by bales of hay and cotton, that the enemies heavy shot might not reach their boilers. Other gunboats were to move down and engage their batteries while the attempt was made to run the fleet past. At 10 o'clock the steam was up, the men on board and all was ready. Slowly they moved out from shore and down the stream. I confess I never expected to see men or boats again. The enemy had on the high bluffs several guns of a hundred and twenty pound caliber and a gun that threw red hot shot and the shores were lined with field artillery.

The river here makes a sharp bend in the form of a horse shoe, allowing the guns to sweep the river far above and below the town. We watched with breathless anxiety as the moment went by. We had not long to wait; we calculated the time it would take the boats to get within range of the enemies guns. A flash as of lightning lit up the sky. Then the thunder tones of a heavy gun fairly shook the earth and echoed from bluff to bluff. Again and again they came thicker and faster until the heavens were buried with one continual flash, and the reports came so fast that they could not be distinguished one from the other. This continued for half an hour, then all was still. Had the fleet gone to the bottom? Or was she in the hands of the enemy? All was in doubt and many wild speculations flew from tent to tent.

For several days before the Sappers and Miners had been busy laying pontoons across the byous bridging the streams and corduroying the swamps and forming a road to pass the troops south across the peninsula to the right of Vicksburg to form a junction with the fleet if she succeeded in passing the blockade.

Along this new highway a system of signal stations were established so that messages could be sent from below to the army above in a few moments, and 'twas by this means we learned that the fleet lay at anchor far below the blockade, having lost but one boat.

Upon this new road the Army of the Tennessee was put in motion on the 22nd day of April. The weather had now become extremely warm and most of the soldiers threw their overcoats and blankets away to lighten their burdens as much as possible. We went on a forced march past the low lands opposite Vicksburg the first day when we came upon high and dry grounds in some of the most beautiful country I ever saw. The corn was now three feet high, quite surprising to us Northerners for the time of the year and everything was in bloom. Some times we would go for a mile between two hedges of climbing roses, whose rich perfume would remind one of the Garden of Eden rather than rebeldom where the principal traffic was in human beings. Then we would come to beautiful lakes, splendid parks, and some of the most elegant mansions, far exceeding anything I had seen at the north, from which the inhabitants had fled.

Through delightful country we moved rapidly for two days when we struck New Carthage, but had to continue the march 70 miles farther by a circuitous route as far as Hard Times, which is below Grand Gulf, on account of the limited means to cross the river.

At Hard Times we came up to the fleet which had now run the blockade at Vicksburg and also at Grand Gulf. The boats had seen hard usage and had been disabled, some sunk, but enough were left to transport the army across and defend against any attack from the shore.

After burying the dead from the boats the work of crossing the stream was begun, the gunboats keeping a sharp lookout both above and below that no hostile foe might approach. It required several days to bring up the trains and light artillery, and it was not until the 26th that the army had fully crossed.

While the maneuvers were going on, Sherman had been thundering away above Vicksburg as a feint to attract their attention until a lodgment should be effected on the east bank of the river; then he was to withdraw his troops and push rapidly forward over the same road we had come.

Not waiting for Sherman's arrival, McPherson with his Seventeenth Corps, pushed boldly out in a southeasterly direction up over the high hills that line the eastern banks of the Mississippi taking no trains except a few ammunition wagons and struck the enemy at Port Gibson.

BATTLE OF PORT GIBSON

The firing began as early as 8 o'clock on the morning of the 21st. The advance cavalry had come up with several detachments of the enemy, but found little difficulty in driving them back until within a mile of the city when the main body was encountered. The day was hot and we moved slow, and when the firing began we came to a halt, each man seeking the shade for a moment to cool off a bit before our days work began. Thus we were loitering on either side of the road, listening to the boom of guns in front of us, and speculating on the prospects of the day, when General McPherson and his staff came galloping up, whom the boys loudly cheered. He was not long in arranging the details of an attack and disposing of the troops. The enemy was strongly posted on the opposite side of a large field behind a deep ravine. Across this ravine the main road ran on a sort of ridge which spanned the ravine as a natural bridge; and back of this defile was a large block house which was filled from cellar to garret with their "sharp shooters" whose deadly aim picked off many of our boys at long distances. On either side of this fortress their lines of infantry were posted, strongly guarding the narrow passage across the ravine. General Logan's third division was placed in the center and ordered to carry the block house, if possible. We formed in the center of the field and moved to the assault. The 45th Illinois attempted to force their way across, but the boys could not stand the withering fire, many were killed; they broke their ranks and fell back. Other regiments took their place but none could withstand the shower of lead that was hurled back upon them. Our Regiment being farther to the left, were battling with the enemy across the ravine while these assaults on the block house were being made and our loss was not heavy. Ben Harford, our drum Major, displayed great courage on this occasion by bringing off the wounded far in advance of the lines. Finding the block house could not be carried by a direct assault of the infantry some heavy field guns were ordered up, which shelled the citadel for more than half an hour, making logs and shingles fly in all directions but failing to set fire to the nest or dislodge the hornets within.

In the meantime General McPherson had dismounted, and throwing a blanket over his shoulders, that his uniform might not attract bullets, came to the front unattended, and being a good engineer, looked the ground carefully over; when he said he believed he had hit on a plan that would win.

Under a tremendous fire of artillery on the block house, he directed the 20th Illinois to crawl along the edge of the ravine, which we did without loss, then letting ourselves down by boughs or grapevines we finally reached the bottom unobserved. Then by the "right flank" we went into them with a will, striking them left and rear before they knew what was coming. Whole companies laid down their arms. One "reb" Captain, when he found himself cut off from escape and between two fires, was so terrified that he took off his hat and quietly walked up to Captain Stevens and delivered him his sword, supposing him to be the commanding General.

Thus in twenty minutes after the old Twentieth had reached the bottom of that ravine they had carried the block house which had been a bone of contention all day and taken nearly 300 prisoners.

Finding their block house gone and their position turned, they fled in all directions and left us masters of the situation. At this point General Grant appeared on the field, evincing the profoundest gratification at the turn of events, and respectfully raised his hat to the 20th Regiment in recognition of their gallant conduct.

Next morning we entered the city, but not to stay, for we were moved steadily on to other conquests. As we passed through the main street of the city, men, women and children filled the walks or gazed anxiously from the upper story windows, as though a monster show had come to town.

Our bands played some of their most lively music, and our flags could be seen floating in the breeze for miles along the road. The negroes grinned and showed "de white ob de eye" to one another, and many a young buck left his all and followed for several days.

Thus our Vicksburg campaign had opened splendidly, and thus far had been a success. The next thing with Grant was to effect a junction with Sherman; at the same time keep the enemy in ignorance of the real destination of the Army. So from Port Gibson we were moved rapidly across Byou Pier in a northerly direction, while the cavalry were sent as far as the Big Black to make feint at the fords, then to the east, etc., until Sherman's arrival which took place a few days later when our colors were pointed in the direction of Jackson, the State Capital, where it was supposed Joe Johnson and his army lay.

BATTLE OF RAYMOND

Our movements now were rapid; the roads good, and the weather a little cooler. We moved by three roads. The 17th Corps on the extreme right, with Logan's Third Div. in the lead.

We found little time to eat, much less to sleep, but were pushed forward before we had time to make a little coffee in the morning; or should we stretch out on the ground at night we had to sleep with one eye open, as the command might be "forward" at any moment.

We were moving along quite rapidly one moonlight night, when one of our boys saw something rolled up in a blanket in the corner of the fence. Wishing to have a little fun, he dodged out of the ranks and giving the bundle a kick exclaimed "Hello, old fellow! Where did you get your whiskey?" At that time some one shied up and said "Look out, that's General Sherman!" The soldier flew back to the ranks in an instant, and was careful how he kicked the next man before he knew who he was.

At 1 o'clock on the 9th of May we came up with the enemy at Raymond, a city of about 10,000 inhabitants, to the southwest of Jackson about 25 miles. Our Third Division was deployed across the main road leading to the town, and stretched across a large cotton field over which we moved down into some timber which grew along a stream which was then nearly dry. Some batteries were planted on either side of the road and began shelling the timber before our arrival, to which the "Rebs" replied with spirit with their guns on the opposite side of the timber near the town.

We rested on our arms in the edge of this timber for a short time, while our scouts reconnoitered their position. Some of their cavalry appeared on our right, but a few bullets hastily drove them back.

Then came the "Rebel Yell," the timber was swarming with them. Then they rushed forward on a charge, and our lines met them bravely; not yielding and inch, I could see a line of continuous fire but a few feet in front of us in the timber. The battle was now <u>fierce.</u> Almost hand to hand, so close were they, that some of our boys fixed their bayonets ready to stab them. Both lines stood equally firm; both equally determined as a couple of bull dogs engaged in a <u>death struggle</u>. The air was full of hissing bullets; they cut up the ground and made the dust fly in our rear as though a heavy shower of hail was falling.

General Logan at the opening of the battle had donned a cloak to conceal his rank, rode along the lines shouting to those who would fall back "For God's sake men, don't disgrace your country; see how they're holding them!"

Robert Darrow dropped his gun and crawled behind a tree, and when I remonstrated he said, "Oh Sergeant, I'll soon be a dead man." He was shot through the lung, and before the battle was over, a cannon ball struck the poor fellow on the knee and he soon died. Our boys were suffering so badly that they crouched down to the ground to avoid the flying missiles of death which filled the air; loading and firing as rapidly as possible on the knee, and 'twas in this position that our Captain Victor H. Stevens was shot in the head and instantly killed.

For two hours this deadly conflict lasted, neither party gaining ground, but continuously losing the life-blood of their men. Our regiment was suffering severely, but there was no thought of giving up. Seeing the hard time our boys were having on account of our exposed position, Colonel Richards ordered the boys to jump over a rail fence which was a few feet to our rear, that the rails might be a little protection against the bullets; but in executing this move, a number of the boys were shot, and among the number was our own Colonel Richards, who was instantly killed.

While this sanguinary conflict was going on, General McPherson had formed the balance of his Corps in line of battle and planted his cannon on a ridge half a mile to our rear, expecting that our Division would be driven back every moment. But as two hours had passed and we still held on, he sent the 18th Wisconsin to our relief. As soon as the fresh troops came up we doubled our lines, fixed our bayonets and going forward with a yell, we soon swept the field, the enemy retreating through their town on the "double quick" and made off in the direction of Jackson, our cavalry in hot pursuit.

This was the severest fighting we had seen thus far, and although not a general engagement, and scarcely mentioned in history; yet seldom in any engagement was the loss greater in proportion to the numbers engaged than on that bloody field at Raymond. I passed over the field soon after the firing had ceased, and the dead were strewn thickly over a space of about ten acres; behind every tree, in every hollow, or behind every log some poor fellow had crawled away and died. The "rebs" had gone and left their wounded in their haste and their moans filled the air as they lay uncared for in the field. One poor fellow called feebly to me as I passed along - he was lying on his back with a bullet hole through his breast - and says, "Sergeant, do you think I'll die?" I told him I hoped he would not, gave him a drink from my canteen and hurried on; as our troops were moving.

We encamped in a graveyard that night, upon a hill near the town. Rather a gloomy place, yet we saw no ghosts, but slept soundly. The next day we moved on in the direction of Jackson. Rain came on and continued during the afternoon and all night. We had no shelter, and to lie on ground with the water underneath and the rain pouring down on us, was not so pleasant. I found a good corner of the fence, put two rails across, then stretched myself on the rails and covering myself with a rubber blanket, and said to myself, "let it rain, who cares," and in this position I slept soundly all night.

CAPTURE OF JACKSON

The morning of the 12th we were on the road bright and early. By nine o'clock we could hear the distant thunder of Sherman's guns near the seat of operations for the day - Jackson.

We were yet a number of miles in the rear, and there seemed to be no particular hurry in getting us up. Perhaps they thought we had done our share already and would give Billy a whack at them first. We were on a different road, and would strike the city from the west; while Sherman's corps was moving up from the south.

We did not get in sight of the enemy until 2 o'clock, at which time it was raining hard and we feared we could not handle our arms. Nevertheless, we were moved right up in front of their breastworks and prepared to make an assault. At this moment 'twas discovered that there were no fortifications a little farther to the north, and to this opening we went on the "double quick." Here McPherson massed his infantry sixteen columns deep and swept down on them past the seminary, sweeping all before him. Sherman also had broken their lines on the south and was pressing hard from that quarter, and by four o'clock the enemy had retreated across the Pearl River, burned the bridge behind them, and the city was ours. The place was sacked by the cavalry and many of the public buildings burned, and the army under Johnson completely routed.

After the fall of Jackson the entire army faced westward, Sherman keeping to the north, McPherson the center, and McClernerd the south. We moved west from Jackson along the railway and camped on the 13th near Bolton. Our rations had now given out and there was no hope of obtaining more until we could open communications with the fleet above Vicksburg, and to do this would require much hard fighting. We had been moved so rapidly that we had little opportunity to forage off the country, and it had been run over so much by the Southern Army there was little left. And when we went in camp on the night of the 13th weary from the long days march, with nothing but some flour captured at Jackson with no means of cooking it, there was much grumbling. For two days we fasted and 'twas no use now to holler "Bread or blood" for the officers could not furnish the bread, but the blood we were getting.

BATTLE OF CHAMPION'S HILL

On the 16th we came up with the enemy strongly posted at a place called Champion's Hill. As General McClernerd's Corps were in the lead, he engaged the enemy long before we came up. The battle had been severe all the forepart of the day, and our troops had suffered much in trying to dislodge them from their strong position on the hills.

Our Division was deployed on the right of the lines about 11 o'clock on ground which was clear of all timber, and we moved up to the brow of a ridge, beyond which the ground gradually descended down to a small stream which cut a deep channel through the low meadow land. Then back of this ground rose another ridge along which we could see their lines stretching along as far as the eye could reach.

As soon as we came into line, our batteries opened fire on their batteries on the opposite side of the field and quite a lively cannonade was kept up for some time while we lay down on the field and took breath.

General Grant made his headquarters at a house about a quarter of a mile back of the lines; and with his perfect system of signals could watch every part of the field as closely, and give his orders as intelligently as though he was everywhere present. So we watched the movements on that field during our fifteen minutes rest; and 'twas surprising to see the rapidity and exactness so vast an army could be handled. Orderlies flew with lightning speed from one part of the field to another. Guns were unlimbered in one place, deliver a few shots, then fly to a better position; ammunition wagons were hurried up to supply the missiles of death; while ambulances were strung along to receive the wounded.

We were now face to face with Pemberton's entire army. Our three corps were also on the ground, and the prospect before us was a greater battle. The boys were in excellent spirits, though desperately hungry, and some even declared they would eat a "Reb before night."

General Logan must have found some whiskey somewhere for he was quite silly for him. When one of Grant's aids rode up to him and asked him where he could be found when the fight began, replied haughtily, "Where the bullets fly the thickest by G_d." When all was ready General Logan rode along the line of his division exhorting something like this:

"Boys, we have got work in front of us. The rascals are all there waiting for us. Now all we want to do is to get at them to make them "git." We always make them "git" when we get at them. You won't have to go alone, I'm going down with you. Now forward; double quick!"

At this the regiments fixed bayonets, and holding their pieces high in the air, went forward with a yell. Our color Sergeant M. Morley, ran so fast with the colors that we had hard work to keep up with him, and keep in any kind of order. Thus we went down the hill on a dead run, right in the teeth of the enemy, never stopping to fire a shot, but pointing our bayonets as though to run them through the enemy rushed right up to them, who had now become terror-stricken at our boldness, crouched down in the channel of the creek, held up their hands and begged for mercy. And right there we took in a whole brigade of Georgia troops.

We did not stop but a moment with our prisoners, but rushed on for the second line a little back of the first on the ridge. We again continued the charge and ceased not to yell as we rushed up the hill. Here we meet some opposition and we emptied our guns into their ranks and rushed on as though nothing had happened. Their ranks break before us and they begin to scatter. Some of the boys rush for a battery at the brow of the hill, mount the horses and come galloping back with guns and all, swinging their hats.

As their ranks broke, their men went panic stricken across the fields into the woods hotly pursued by as many live Yankees as there were fleeing "rebs" each Yankee intent on gobbling as many prisoners as possible.

When we had chased them half a mile or more a halt was called, and looking round I saw we were far past the main body of the enemy, for the hill proper was yet literally covered with them. But we had completely annihilated their left wing, and outflanked them so effectually that they made a hasty retreat from their stronghold on the hill and left us masters of the field with about 3000 prisoners.

Then the boys of our brigade brought in their prisoners from the chase, scarcely any one came back without two or three prisoners and one little old Dutchman of our company by the name of Jahle came strutting back with eight. We "corralled" our prisoners, put a guard over them, and had a time of general rejoicing for the next half hour. After which we began to feel the pangs of hunger again, as we had had nothing scarcely for the last two days.

I picked out a clean looking "Reb" who had been shot down, and whose carcass lay stretched at full length on the grass, sat down beside him, and from his well filled haversack of corn bread and beef, made a sumptuous meal. When dinner was over I rolled the fellow over, unbuttoned his vest and took from the pocket thereof a copy of the New Testament, richly bound with pasteboard, and read, "If thine enemy hunger, give him to eat; if he thirst, give him to drink," etc. The poor fellow was now obeying the spirit and letter of that command; now, if never before in all his life. Little did that man think when he was so carefully preparing that haversack with 3 days rations, that a "blue-bellied yankee" would devour the contents thereof.

We camped near the field that night, and next day moved down towards the Big Black where McClernerd took in 2500 more of Pemberton's army, and a number of batteries as they were endeavoring to cross. The enemy having destroyed the bridges over the Big Black, gangs of men were put to work during the night of the 17th constructing new ones, and on the morning of the 18th the 17th Army Corps passed over to the west side of that stream. Sherman having a pontoon train, had lain them much sooner than we could build bridges, and had passed his corps over a day in advance, while McClernerd brought up the rear farther to the south.

It will be seen that our corps occupied the center of the Army, hence we moved along the Jackson road which runs due east from Vicksburg over a high ridge road and 1/2 a mile north from the railroad tracks. We had some heavy skirmishing along this road; but by the night of the 18th we had the enemy all run inside their fortifications, and we bivouaced within half a mile of their outer works in line of battle, our Regiment on the side of a deep ravine whose banks were so steep, as I remember I had to straddle a small tree to keep from falling down. Yet in this position, I enjoyed a most refreshing sleep. The next morning we moved up within range of their works, which were now enveloped in smoke, as they had set fire to a number of buildings that stood outside, to prevent our using them for the purpose of sharp shooting.

ASSAULT ON THE WORKS

General Grant relying on the demoralized condition of the enemy, from their many defeats outside their works, thought it possible to carry them by a direct assault. Accordingly arrangements were made for a simultaneous attack at 2 o'clock on the 19th, all along the line. At the firing of two heavy guns as a signal, the entire army moved forward to the assault and the battle soon became general and raged with great fury until night put an end to the conflict.

The enemy had a continuous line of works, from the mouth of the Yazoo on the north extending back from the city 3/4 of a mile around to the Mississippi on the south. On each high point of ground along this line they had built strong forts with cannon to sweep along the rifle pits, and every open space in front. Along in front of this line the ground was cut up by deep chasms filled with standing or fallen timber, so that the movements of troops was extremely difficult and irregular.

All that afternoon we manoeuvered back and forth through these difficult passes, but only to receive a murderous fire from their rifle pits whenever we exposed ourselves to view. Some times we would get close up to their works, and we even planted our colors on the outer slope of one of their parapets, but of what avail; they were perfectly secure in their trenches, to cross which we could not; we could only occasionally pick off a "Reb" when he showed his head above their works.

At night we sought more sheltered positions and bivouaced along the sides of the ravines, but in easy range of their works, and a continuous fire was kept up during the night. All the 20th and 21st was spent in placing the artillery in commanding positions, and opening communication with the fleet now laying at Hains Bluff by which we were to obtain our supplies of "Hard Tack" which we stood in great need of, as we had subsisted for twenty days on seven days rations.

SECOND ASSAULT

On the afternoon of the 21st, General Grant issued his orders for a second attack on the works, to begin simultaneously from all points at 10 o'clock on the morning of the 22nd. Our position on the morning of the 22nd was on a high ridge over which the Jackson road ran directly up to what is called Fort Hill. This was built on a high and commanding position, rising about twenty feet above the ground, whose guns had a good sweep of the field far to the right and left in front of their rifle pits. Our Brigade was drawn up in front of this fort early in the day, and to our left was placed a battery of thirty-two pound howitzers designed to batter down the walls of the fort while we were to make the attempt to carry it by storm. We moved down the road by the right flank at 10 o'clock, and when within five rods of the fort, we were met by a murderous fire from their parapet, their guns having a fair sweep of the road. In this fire many were killed, among whom was my friend Lars Olsen who fell mortally wounded and was carried back by his brother Neals, who when he got him back to where he could be attended to, hastily rejoined his Company.

The boys crouched down by the bank alongside this road which afforded a partial shelter, while the large guns belched their heavy iron missiles against the fort, which made the dirt and timber fly in all directions. Finding we could make no farther advance in this direction, we fell back under the heavy guns where we lay for more than an hour, while the combined artillery of that part of the field was concentrated on that one fort. During the cannonade a shell burst as she left the gun (called rotten shell) and wounded fifteen men out of our Regiment.

From our position here, we could see the fierce assaults of General Ransom to our right, as he stormed the rifle pits, but again and again driven back with heavy loss. All along the line the battle raged with great fury, and one continuous roar of artillery shook the very earth from morning until night.

Again we made an attempt on Fort Hill. We moved from our position farther around to our left on the double quick to where there is an open space of ground; here we face the east bastion and make a rush for the base of the fort on a dead run amid a shower of lead that was hurled down upon us. We were the only Regiment that succeeded in reaching this position, and as I believe, without the loss of a man.

We plant our colors on the side of the fort, but could go no farther as the side was almost perpendicular, and to climb up its sides would be hard to do without opposition; but with a row of bayonets at the top waiting to receive us, who would attempt it? To go back, we might lose half our men. We were in a bad fix indeed. We hugged the ground at the base of the fort; we climb up a few feet and burrow ourselves into its sides to avoid their enfilading fire and remain there the rest of the day. Towards night we began to get hungry, as well as to suffer greatly from thirst, from the constant biting of cartridges that filled our mouths with powder, and our canteens were all empty.

While wondering thereabout what we should do, who should we see but "Black Ben" coming across the field towards us. Ben had taken in our dilemma from his position behind the hill. He knew we would be suffering by this time from hunger and thirst. So Ben, our Ben who liked the boys, took his life in his hand, a camp kettle of coffee on his woolley head, strapped some sacks of hard-tack around his body, and started across the field. They fire at him from the fort, the balls made the dirt fly around him, but Ben undismayed presses forward. He dare not run, he would spill his coffee and the boys would get none. At last Ben reaches our line and deposits his load at our feet, and oh, how his eyes shone as the boys covered his head with praises, filled his pockets with tobacco, and greedily devoured our meal. The battle had raged fiercely all day along the entire line, but no decided advantage gained by the Union troops but the loss was far greater than on any other day during the Vicksburg campaign. Many had fallen so near the works that their bodies could not be got at; were never buried; their bones were found after the surrender where they fell.

When it was dark, and the roar of battle had subsided, we managed to get a company of a dozen negroes up to where we lay with picks and shovels, to dig us some trenches, that we might be more secure in our position, but the noise of their picks were heard inside the fort, and the first we knew, a volley came down on us which killed six of the negroes, and the work had to be abandoned.

Before 'twas fairly light next morning we skulked slyly back to our old position from which we started the day before; thus ending a terrible battle without any gain farther than demonstrating the fact that the works could not be taken by direct assault, and all further attempts were abandoned.

From this on we settled down to a regular siege. We built counter works on every available spot all around theirs, behind which we erected our tents, put logs on top of our defenses to protect our heads, under which we had a line of port-holes where we could sit and pop away all day with perfect safety. Men were kept at their work all the time, and if a hat was seen above their works 'twould be instantly riddled with bullets. So the shooting was kept up night and day, and as the days wore on we became so accustomed to the whistle of bullets that we paid little attention to them, and often the boys would expose themselves in the most reckless manner.

All this time the fleet was not idle. Every day they would move down and engage the water batteries, or send their huge shell crashing into town. At night during these bombardments we would watch the great shell as they would rise from the mortar boats in the river, and with a loud buzzing noise, rise high in the air above the city, leaving a trail of fire in their path, then descending, burst with thunder tones and send its fragments in all directions. During these bombardments, the inhabitants would leave their houses and go into caves they had dug previously in the sides of the hills.

But this shelling was not all on one side. The enemy had mortars too; and some times they would become exceedingly annoying. About half a mile to our left behind their parapet, they planted a large mortar that threw a hundred pound shell. For many days this particular gun tried to drop into our camp. Our Regiment was on the side of a ravine and unless a ball should drop down perpendicular could not reach us; so most of these shell went beyond doing little harm aside from tearing up the ground and keeping us constantly on the lookout. I had made on the side of the ravine a nice little bed of canes on which I used to sleep soundly; but one night I was awakened by a loud rumbling noise, and looking up saw directly over my head, a huge shell which burst at that instant and sent its fragments crashing all through the camp, but strange to say, no one was hurt.

COON SKIN BILL

There was a fellow who wore a coon skin cap - said to have been brought up on the Plains among the cowboys - at any rate, he was as bold and daring a young man as one would wish to see. He claimed to have gone into the rebel camp as a spy and brought back much valuable information to the commanding general. Also to have made his escape from Andersonville when taken there a prisoner.

Well, Bill being full of energy as well as daring deeds, and wishing still farther to grow in fame, assured the general if he would be allowed, and might have a little help, he would look right into Fort Hill, would give its strength and arrangement, and could tell just where 'twould be safe to make an attack. Well, Bill set to work on an eminence before the fort to build his tower, and as it rose higher and higher, the "Rebs" tried to batter it down with their guns, but Bill and his tower kept going up, and they never succeeded in hitting it, though at close range. When about 40 feet high, Bill placed some large mirrors, so that by reflection he could see the enemy without raising his head above the top of his tower, which if he did, would make a fine mark for the sharp shooters. Thus Bill could look down into their fort and see their movements; but whether any real good came of the thing, I never knew.

We worked like beavers, pushing our works up to theirs as close as possible. In some places there would be simply a bank of earth between us and at such places we had to be very cautious how we raised our heads.

When night would come on, and the firing slacken, it was not an uncommon thing to hear the boys talking to the "Reb" boys in the most friendly manner, something as follows:

"Halloo there, 'reb'; how are you tonight?"

"Pretty well Yank, how are you?"

"How many men have you got over there?"

"About a hundred thousand; enough to lick all the blue-bellied Yankees in all God's creation."

These conversations would generally end in the "Rebs" asking the Yankee if he had any coffee to trade for Confederate Script when an armistice would be agreed on, and the boys would meet between the lines, make their trades, have a friendly chat and return to their posts again.

FORT HILL

About the middle of June General McPherson determined to blow up

Fort Hill, which was now supposed to be the Gibraltar of their entire system of forts. Accordingly a deep trench was dug wide enough to pass six files of soldiers abreast. The trench was run up to the base of the fort with a row of "gabions" on each side to protect the men while at work. Then a gang of miners was put to work who ran a drift down under the fort until they reached its center. Then 40 kegs of giant powder was deposited in this excavation connected to a fuse, and its mouth filled up. When all was ready our Brigade was drawn up along the trench as near as prudence would allow, and instructed to charge into the fort if possible, as soon as the mine should explode.

About 3 o'clock p.m., the troops being in readiness, the trail was fired, and in a few minutes the very earth shook beneath our feet, and such a mass of earth went heavenward as I had never seen before. All was dark with the clouds of smoke and dust; then came crashing down to earth again timbers, animals and men in one grand ruin; several bodies came down perfectly nude with every bone broken.

When the smoke cleared away a little, Colonel Smith, at the head of the 45th Illinois Regiment rushed into the crater, but in less than a minute he was brought back a corpse. His men fought desperately and lost heavily, but could not hold out. Then our 20th Illinois rushed in and took their places. We fought our way into the interior of the fort which was now divided into two parts with a bank of earth about 6 feet high, dividing the open space back of which the enemy had hastily massed his forces. We gained this bank and some of the boys wanted to go over in their midst, but most thought it would be folly, as we would only go to certain death and nothing be accomplished. So we stood at the bank as many as could, and would raise our guns up at arms length and fire down among them on the opposite side, while others were busy loading our guns and passing them up. Thus a continuous fire was poured in upon them, but whether to any effect, we could not tell, but they were there all the same, for we could see the flash of their guns, and hear the whistle of their bullets.

After this random firing had been going on for some time, hand grenades were brought in to us which we would light and throw over among them, and the fight continued in this manner until dark, when we were relieved and the 23rd Indiana went in to take our place.

After dark the enemy brought up loaded bombs which they would throw over the embankment and explode them in the midst of our boys, with telling effect, who were huddled together in the crater, and 'twas then the most fearful carnage commenced.

The exploding shell would mangle the bodies of the boys of the 23rd most fearfully, and a constant stream were being brought back with arms and legs blown off, and some with their bowels gushing out, bleeding and mangled in all conceivable forms. This was kept up until 9 o'clock, when finally it was of no use to send men into the crater to be slaughtered and no prospect of holding more than a part of the fort, the troops were withdrawn and the undertaking abandoned.

From this on there was no hard fighting at Vicksburg, although the fleet continued to shell the town, and the crack of the rifle could always be heard along the line of the works; yet, there was no farther effort made by either side but simply to hold its own, and we enjoyed for many a day comparative quiet.

Near the last of June they made a salley in the night, and endeavored to break through our lines, but were easily driven back. Sherman having now withdrawn his corps, moved back to the Big Black to watch the movements of Johnson, who was now at Jackson with the intention of raising the siege, and we had settled down to a state of quiet and rest behind our breastworks, and did not care if such a state of things should continue all the rest of the summer.

PART IV

Occupation Army

THE SURRENDER

On the morning of July 3rd, as I was leisurely walking far around to the right of our lines to make some purchases of a sutler who was stationed there, I was a little surprised to see a group of "Rebs" standing on top their parapet with no guns in their hands, looking towards us as though they wanted to say something.

I was near a Wisconsin Regiment and I called to some of the boys to see the rebs; and up went a dozen heads from the game of cards in which they were engaged, who on seeing the Southerners standing out so boldly, we all made a scramble to get on our works too. Then a shell came crashing down past us, and of course we all dodged, when they laughed and said we ought not to dodge our own shell.

We had quite a friendly talk with them, of whom we learned the true state of affairs inside their works. They said we could never have gotten them out by fighting, but hunger had conquered them. They were a noble looking set of men, but the traces of famine were plainly depicted upon their countenance; and had I been at my own regiment, I would gladly have gone and got them something to eat.

But I hastened back to my regiment, and as I passed along the line the white flag floated from every stronghold, and the firing which had been kept up for more than forty days had entirely ceased.

Then General Pemberton came out unattended, and met General Grant in front of our position down near Fort Hill, under the shade of an oak tree - ever since called Pemberton Oak - and there the men were in earnest conversation all that day.

Early on the morning of the 4th, the "Rebs" came out by detachments and stacked their arms when we moved into the city and celebrated our "fourth" inside the works. It was the warmest day of the season when we entered town, and the boys sought the wells in quest of drink. We had not seen the face of a woman for six weeks, and the first one we came across was an old peaked-nose hag who poked her head out of an upper story window, as some of the boys were entering her yard for drink, and exclaimed, "Don't you insult me; don't you dare to do it, you villains, I want none of ye around my house!" Some of the boys told her she was not worth insulting, but the "don't you do it'" was kept up as long as there was a man in sight.

The first few days in town I spent, while not on duty, inspecting things about the city. There were over two hundred cases of arms that had never been used stored away, eighty pieces of field artillery, in fact implements of war enough to equip a small army. The buildings had been thoroughly riddled by shell and the marks of war were everywhere visible. The inhabitants were in a famishing condition, and when we opened a bakery where we made fresh bread for our regiment, the women, those too who had been wealthy before, would come out and beg a loaf as we carried it through the streets.

When our prisoners had all been paroled and sent home, the work of arranging and governing the affairs of the town was begun. A large staff was erected at the Court House on which the Stars and Stripes was run up; and steamers began to ply the river unmolested between Cairo and New Orleans. The citizens at first crabbed, soon began to like the new state of affairs as trade revived, money became plenty and order and quiet prevailed.

But the month of August was a trying one for us Northerners. The weather was so hot that we had to lie and sleep during the day and could only venture out after the sun bad gone down. Everything dried up and the ground was full of large gaping cracks. Many of the troops got sick with fevers, and the hospitals were full to overflowing. There was now a perfect lull in military operations. I amused myself part of the time playing chess, as I found a valuable set of ivories in their old barracks, and part of the time sitting in the shade drawing pictures.

By the first of September we began to have some refreshing showers and the weather became more endurable, and at the same time the boys, many of them, began to recover from their illness, and we began to enjoy life better than ever, especially the life of the soldier. Many of the families began to return to their homes, who went away before the siege began, and we formed many acquaintances among them, whom we found to be noble and generous people.

There were several fine churches in town, but I always attended the M.E. Church, which was some times presided over by our Army Chaplain, and some times by their regular pastor, a southern man. We formed a choir, composed of several soldiers, Miss Jennie Hammett, and two Miss Longs of Vicksburg. Our leader was a young doctor who had lately been discharged from the Confederate Army where he served as an Ensign. We had bulley times as we would meet in some of the high-toned houses for rehearsals, and bulley music we made.

Howard Stephens, a member of our Company, and a fifer for the Regiment, had a particular fancy for young ladies, for which Vicksburg was famed. There were girls of every hue, from the snowy white who done nothing all day but sit in the shade and fan herself and keep the mosquitos off, to the patent skinned wench who worked in the field and lived on corn bread, drank sour milk and chewed tobacco.

Well, Howard would go round town, call at some of the most respectable houses, and addressing the lady say "Madam, I've called to pay my respects to your daughter!" And if told they had no daughter, he would say: "Oh, excuse me, I must have made a mistake; perhaps 'tis in the next house, they have a daughter, have they not?" In this way he would find out where the lovely maidens were. And oh, my, the first thing I knew Howard was enquiring around where he could borrow a boiled shirt, and that very night the fellow went off and got married to a southern girl, but I never heard of his taking her home with him.

THE "CITY OF MADISON"

was a large steamer in the government employ. She lay at the docks of Vicksburg in plain sight of our camp and not a quarter of a mile away, while a gang of laborers were busily engaged stowing her hold and decks with heavy shell and other munitions of war for the southern ports.

When the work was nearly complete, and she was heavily loaded with shell and thousands of boxes of cartridges, the boat through some accident blew up, shaking the town to its very foundations. The report was so loud that it looked dark for a moment; when I looked, the air was filled with flying missiles; the hurricane deck, the cabins and all the upper part of the ship was flying through the air, then came crashing down. As soon as the smoke cleared away, scarcely a remnant of her was to be seen. The houses along the levee were a complete wreck, and the crowd eagerly rushed down to the water to see the sight and help the wounded, but nothing was found of the three ladies who were in the cabin, or but few of the crew who were loading the boat at the time of the accident.

COLORED BALL

When on patrol duty one night, we were attracted by the lively music and the brilliantly lighted hall, to where the young and giddy of Vicksburg's colored society were making merry to the music of the trombone and horn. Friend Garner and I entered the hall about 11 o'clock, taking good care to keep near an open window, as the peculiar perfume which nature had given them was not so agreeable on a warm night, especially when heated in the dance. We soon found we were not at a plantation cabin where the festive darkey dances the "juby" at night by the music "ob de banjo on de bones," but at a real genuine city ball, where the sea of broadcloth and silk moved as gracefully as the gentle billows which are stirred by a summers breeze. This kind of society would not "sociate" wid de common niggers;" and if one should poke his woolly head in that hall, he would be ruthlessly "fired." So this society was kept pure and free from all the contaminating influence of rowdyism.

The hall contained about 40 couples of the "elete" of negro society, who were gaily skipping in the giddy mazes of the dance, and their color was as varied in hue as the clothes they wore on that momentous occasion. They came to us often and asked us to dance, but we declined on account of not being dressed for company; then as though they thought we felt above them, they would inform us that they were no <u>black niggers</u>, a term they would always use to express their respectability.

But the greatest curiosity of this particular occasion was the queer antics of the young ladies as they moved backwards and forth to the stirring music with several yards of trail thrown over the left arm while with their white kidded right they would dart it forth to their partners as though 'twas a snake ready for a bite. Their faces always wore a smile, and the pearly teeth were everywhere visible set in a background of the darkest ebony. Their movements were indeed graceful, their bodies swaying with the music, while their feet were as accurate in time as could be kept by an experienced drummer boy.

We asked one young lady, whose skin was white as snow, and in whose veins probably not a particle of African blood could be found, why she did not associate with those of her own color? When she said she never knew any other society, was sold into slavery when a child and counted as one of the colored.

ON THE BIG BLACK

On the first of October, our Brigade, now commanded by Brg. Gen. Force, consisting of the 23rd Indiana, 20th Iowa, and 20th and 124th Illinois Regiments, were sent out to occupy the country east of the city along the line of Big Black river.

We selected a good camping ground on that stream near the confluence of a large creek and the river, where the ground was high and dry, and close to a large field where we had our battalion drills and held our "dress parades."

The ground around our camp was sparsely covered with oaks along the stream, then farther back the forest became more dense with here and there a clearing for a small farm.

Our regiment was now quite small, mustering less than five hundred, commanded by Colonel Bradley, who was by this time liked quite well by the boys, and acknowledged by all to be an efficient officer. Since Steven's death, our Co. "H" had been commanded by John McEowen. Some recruits had been sent us from time to time, but not as many as had fallen by disease or in battle. We were now fourteen miles from Vicksburg, being connected by Railroad, which ran a train twice a day, brought out our supplies, and took us back and forth whenever we wished to go. Here we slicked up the grounds around our camps, put bunks in all our tents, and prepared to pass the winter as agreeably as possible. There was no village near us, and but for a few cabins scattered here and there, we would have been quite in the wilderness.

So when we had got well settled in our new camp, and not wishing to become altogether uncivilized on account of our isolation a few of us got together and concluded we would build a church. Getting a permit from Colonel Bradley, and a score of axes from our Quartermaster, we soon made the Southern Forest ring with the falling of trees and the shouts of laughter. Our Chaplain was with the boys working might and main in his shirt sleeves, and he stated emphatically that he never built a church under so favorable circumstances, or with so little difficulty to obtain subscriptions. Then the mules were put to work and logs were snaked in from all quarters, and in a few days we had a splendid edifice, a much better church than I had ever known soldiers to build before. We covered our edifice with a huge tent, built a log fireplace with a stick chimney at one end, then splitting some logs in half we made pews, and with a barrel for a pulpit, we were ready for business.

The following Sunday we gave the thing a grand dedication. Every log was occupied as our minister took his text behind that barrel, while a rousing fire blazed in the great fireplace at the end. Some of the boys had come down from the 23rd Indiana and filled every vacant place, so Black Ben had to peek in at the door. Our preacher held this vast audience spell bound until nearly noon; when some one down in camp shouted "grub pile," when the whole congregation broke for the door, and went shouting down the hill like a lot of starved wolves after a flock of sheep.

In the afternoon we held our regular Sunday School, when several "big infant" classes were organized with mother Buck of our Co. "M" as principal. All winter long our chaplain dealt out the Gospel to fine audiences composed of the best people of the 20th Regiment.

On Thursdays we held our regular weekly debates, and on these occasions our Chapel would be crowded, when we would discuss some of the most momentous questions of the day, and would pitch into each other as unmercifully as though we were on a charge of bayonets. Some of the 23rd boys would come over and take part; but they would get mad so easily we had to put them out.

A paper was also published and read in our society, having special reference to the latest news items, especially the social events of Big Black society, whether that society was black society or white, and many a boy went home to his tent vowing 'twas the sharpest thing he ever heard.

BIG BLACK CHAPEL.

URIAH HENDERSON

was a recruit who came to us at Bird's Point. He was a fine strong boy physically, had a fist like a sledge hammer and professed to be able to knock down the best man in the regiment on the slightest provocation; hence all were a little cautious how they crossed his path; for on one occasion I knew him to knock a man bigger than himself, so flat 'twas hard to tell whether he had been shot or a mule kicked him. Uriah had a good mouth for whiskey. When a little toddy was issued to the men, as a preventative against disease, he would sell his rations, his jack-knife, or whatever he had, and gobble up enough to make him staving drunk; then Uriah could be heard far in the night grinding his teeth and saying to himself, "I'm a tough nut; I'm a son-of-a-gun on four wheels." There was something strange about Uriah. He had a peculiar knack of getting sick just as the bullets began to fly; and I have seen him fall to the ground and double himself up as though in the greatest agony, while in his face would show the most horrid contortions, and he would rather have a bayonet run through him than move from his tracks. He was no earthly use as a soldier, and the greatest wonder to me was he was not drummed out of camp long before his time was out.

CHRISTMAS

On this day, for some reason or other, there was an extra allowance of "firewater" issued that would kill at 40 rods, besides the boys of our Company managed to get hold of a keg of beer, and before noon two thirds of the Company were staving drunk, and a general "melee" began. Indeed, most of them were so drunk they could not fight but wallowed around on the ground like a lot of hogs chewing at each others ears. The Captain, scarcely able to walk himself, blustered around as though he was in the heat of battle, and ordered me to call out the Company to quell the riot, which order I had to obey, if it did come from a drunken officer, or subject myself to court martial. So I called together the Company, those who were sober, and got together twelve men fit for duty. There were many more who would not drink a drop, but on this day happened to be on guard, or absent in the City. Then with my 12 men I proceeded according to the Captain's orders to arrest the most boisterous ones and place them in the guard house until sober. We got an ambulance, bound several of them and piled them in. Coming to Uriah, who was by this time crazy, we had to use the bayonet freely to get him to submit, the Captain all the time shouting "Run him through! Run him through!" We finally succeeded in tying the brute and loading him into the wagon; then his wrath changed to wailing and he yelled all the way to the Guard House, "O-o-o, Blanchard I'm dying, roll me out the hind end of the wagon, o-o-o-o." When Uriah was dumped at the Guard House and let loose, he straightened up and doubling up his fist to some of the 23rd boys, says, "You sons of b___, I can lick the best man in the 23rd Indiana."

PART V

Three Years Are Up

RE-ENLISTING

Our three years term was now drawing to a close, consequently the government saw the danger arising if so large a proportion of the army should go home as whose terms would soon expire, especially as those were old and experienced men, able to endure the severest hardships and would not flinch in times of the greatest danger.

Accordingly a bounty of $200 was offered together with a furlough for 30 days, if they would enlist for three years more, or while the war lasted, if not sooner discharged. The bait was a tempting one to one who had had three years of camp life, and had scarcely seen friends or home in the time, then to go for 30 days with $200 in the pocket, how pleasant the thought.

Yet, most of the men had made up their minds to go home the coming Spring, saying they had done their share already, and enlistments went on slow. Speeches were made to our Regiment by our Colonel and by General McPherson himself, of the most patriotic character; and at night bon fires were built, drums beat, songs sang, which together with the unusual amount of whiskey that was drank had raised the spirits of the boys to fever heat, and this way they got most of the boys pledged to stand by the flag and their names enrolled.

As for myself, I had no idea of going home while the war lasted. I considered the Confederacy on its last legs, and a few more vigorous strokes would put an end to its existence, and for the bulk of the army to retire to their homes, might be the means of losing a great deal that had been gained, besides prolonging the war indefinitely. So Neals Olsen and myself were the first to re-enlist in our Company, and most of the boys we persuaded to follow suit, and then we had a long task in making muster out, and muster in Rolls.

PRIZE DRILL

During our stay at Big Black, great pains had been taken to perfect the troops in drill. Indeed, we had little else to do in a military point of view. So during the entire winter battalions were in the field most of the time maneuvering and Colonels were putting their commands through a thorough system of tactics; as the day was rapidly approaching when the different regiments were to compete on the field for a banner offered by the Commanding General. Day after day we done our best in all the different maneuvers laid down in Hardin's Tactics; and great proficiency was made by all the troops at our "post." General Force too would often drill the entire Brigade which made an imposing sight on the field during its maneuvers, but the General most delighted and always closed the day with a grand charge of bayonets while in "echelon."

On the 10th of January our Brigade was drawn up on the plain where the contest was to take place. General Force and staff at the head of the column, and six Judges on horseback were stationed at another part of the field. Then one after another the different regiments went through the manual of arms and various evolutions known to regimental drill in the most perfect manner. The 124th Illinois being a new regiment was full, 1000 strong. They had drawn new suits for the occasion, wore white gloves and their arms shone like polished silver. They had not been shattered by many battles as we had and no raw recruits had been put among them since they came out. Hence their appearance was the finest and their drill could not be surpassed; and they were also declared winners.

MERIDIAN RAID

On the first of February all preparations were made for a long march into the interior of the enemies country, after which we were promised our leave of absence for 30 days. Everything was left intact in our camps, as we expected to return and occupy the grounds again, so we had no tents along, only a few ammunition wagons and provisions for ten days.

We crossed the Big Black on the afternoon of the 2nd, a jolly set of fellows as ever went on the war path. We had had a long rest and the boys felt splendid. As we got well under way and the lines began to lengthen out, the boys could be heard for miles along the line singing:

> "We'r going home
> We'r going home
> We'r going home
> To die no more," &

When this tune got stale,

> John Brown's body lies mouldering in the ground
> John Brown's body lies mouldering in the ground;

and the hallelujahs filled the air and echoed back from every hill top. So we marched and sang, and sang and marched, until we reached Bolton, where we went into camp for the night.

The next day the enemy appeared in our front near the old battle ground of Champion's Hill and after a sharp skirmish was driven back without retarding the progress of the troops to any considerable extent. We moved by three different roads, with our 17th Corps in the center along the line of the railroad on which the enemy directed most his attention and skirmishes was constantly kept up in our front. These lines, on parallel roads with cavalry thrown out on the flanks swept over a strip of country about 40 miles wide, and carried destruction and desolation in its train. The third day out we met the enemy in considerable force who made a stand on the opposite side of a large field with their guns posted so as to sweep the ground for a mile around, while their cavalry were operating on its flanks. We brought a battery into position and tried to dislodge them, while our Brigade was deployed for its support. But the enemies fire was most accurate. Had they practiced on that same ground, they could not have done better. They killed some of the gunners and dismounted a gun in the first few shots, and several batteries had to be brought into position before we could dislodge them. Then a continual skirmish was kept up for eighteen miles, a running fight, a fire and fall back, until we reached Jackson when our advance guard put a finishing stroke to them, taking a number of prisoners and some of their guns. We entered the city on the 9th and succeeded in saving the bridge over the Pearl river before the enemy had time to destroy it.

This was the third time the town had been captured by our men; and the third time their armies had been routed here, and this time a great part of the city was destroyed.

We rested here on the 10th during which time we made the inhabitants sick. They had gathered up all the chickens and carefully concealed them in their houses, and at first not a chick or turkey could be found. George Palm and I thought we "smelt a rat" as we were out searching for some. We went through a fine looking house, and it looked as though chickens had been kept there; so we went round to the back, but could see none. Then we listened at the back door, and sure enough, we heard the sound of chickens within. But how to get at them was the next question. The door was securely locked. We were not long in prying off the lock, and in less than three seconds a coop of three dozen fine chickens was slipping out the back door. Had the chickens kept their mouth shut all would have been well, but some of the old hens insisted on squacking, which thing attracted the attention of the women of the house who came charging out with broom-fire poker screeching, "You villains! You black yankees! You sons of b___!" and it looked as though right then and there would be the fiercest engagement of the war. But all this time the coop kept moving off and soon we were out of reach of our fair opponents, and in less than an hour they were all singing a last lullaby in a great caldron kettle up in the camp of Co. M.

Now as it got abroad how we obtained our poultry, many of the neighboring houses had to suffer, or at least the chickens did, until the camps became filled with them and the day was given up to feasting. In the meantime some soldiers had overhauled a Tobacco Factory, and brought to camp several hundred pounds of choice Killickinnick done up in five pound bags which lasted many days along the road.

We crossed the Pearl River, the beautiful Pearl, on the 11th, and moved by easy marches until we reached Molton, which had been sacked and set on fire by the advance guard. We were now well into the Confederacy, and the work of destruction was fairly under way. Houses, fences, forests, were all in a blaze on either side of us, and everything was left in one grand ruin after the army had passed. Not a depot, bridge or water tank was left on any railroad, and more than 300 miles of track were torn up, the ties piled up and burned, and many of the rails bent and twisted around trees that the work of destruction might be the more complete.

We reached Brandon on the 13th, a fine large town for that section of the country, and quite a railroad center. The roads were destroyed for miles each way and the town was left in ashes. Pushing on we reached Hillsboro where we found a large force under Bragg had been in position intending to give battle, but had wisely concluded not to risk one and withdrew on our approach. We had little fighting along this part of the route; of course guerrillas hung along the flanks and would occasionally pounce upon a foraging party, or pick up stragglers who chanced to fall behind. The nights were cold, and as we had no tents along, and very scanty blankets, it became necessary that the inhabitants should contribute their share towards the comfort of the weary soldiers on these cold nights, and accordingly about 3 o'clock every cabin along the road would be visited by from ten to twenty different soldiers, and every blanket quilt or carpet would disappear from the house; they would be carried to where the army camped, used for the night, and in the morning the camp would be full of women looking for their bedding. At the Tallahatchie, twenty miles from Meridian, we found the roads obstructed by felled trees, and the teams had to be left under guard while the army pushed on to the latter place under great difficulty, through a barren and heavily timbered country, where every house was made of logs, and the ignorant and indolent people lived by fishing and hunting.

BATTLE OF CHUNKEY

At the Tallahatchie General Force with his first Brigade, was sent down to the right to destroy the large Railroad Bridge across that stream at a place called Chunkey, which place we reached after a forced march of two hours.

We found the enemy in considerable force at the bridge ready to dispute our approach. But General Force halted not a moment but moved his men rapidly to the place as though the work had to be done and the sooner the better. We drove in their pickets, then deployed the infantry, and moved rapidly through the timber to the attack, on their lines drawn up near a farm house where they were maintaining a brisk infantry fire. Several of the boys were killed; but when we opened on them they fell back to the bridge sheltering themselves as much as possible behind its timbers and there continued to maintain a galling fire. We soon found we had a hard nut to crack if we continued to fight them in front when the force was divided part working around to their rear while the fire was kept up vigorously in front.

This had the desired effect; they hurried from the east end of the bridge while we set fire to the west end and soon the entire structure was in flames and the enemy was beyond pursuit. Then we returned again to the Army having won a battle, destroyed a half million bridge and got around by the time the horn blew for dinner.

General Hurlburt's Corps were in possession of Meridian when we arrived, and most of the town had already been destroyed. Large gangs of men were out on the railroads north and south tearing up the tracks and burning whatever rolling stock the "Rebs" had not run off.

Their army had evacuated a few hours before. Hurlburt entered and had crossed the Tombigbee and a pursuit was deemed useless. We rested here only one day, and during that time we became so black that a stranger would not have known there was a white man among us. We had burned pitch pine in our camps, and before we knew it the smoke had formed a complete tar on the skin which took many days to get off.

When all was desolation in and around Meridian the return march was begun by a different route, this time farther to the north. During our march of more than 300 miles the army had subsisted almost entirely off the country. Foraging parties were out continually on the flanks scouring the country for whatever would be of value or use to the army, but the inhabitants being warned of our approach would hide whatever of value they had in their swamps in the ground or in cellars, so we had to rely in most cases on information obtained of the negroes.

I was out one day with my regiment on one of those expeditions not far from Meridian; and after traveling a long way, we came across a rather poor looking plantation but 'twas the only one in that neighborhood. As we halted in front of the house the women came out and informed us that the "Rebs" had been there a few days before and stripped them of everything and left them in a starving condition.

Not being satisfied with this statement, we made a thorough search of the place and unearthed enough of fine smoked ham and bacon to fill a large cotton wagon. Then we yoked the oxen hitched to the wagon and drove off and left the women and children crying and screaming in the house. Some times cattle would be found so plentiful that they would be killed only for their tongues and liver, and the rest of the carcass left, but all would be killed that if ever the southern army should pass through that section they would find poor picking. Then again in passing through some of the large pine forests we would go two or three days and find nothing, as a great deal of land in the section was barren and unsettled.

We came across a remnant of a tribe of the old Choctaw Indians who lived in these quarters. We had lots of fun with them; we sat down on the grass in a great circle and smoked the pipe of peace with them. One pipe served the company; this one was immense, filled with part leaf tobacco and part sumac leaf. Each man was allowed three whiffs, then he would pass it to his next neighbor who would take three whiffs, and so on, the great pipe would travel around that circle. When asked which side they were on, the north or the south, they would reply "We no fight; we all peace." When nearing the Pearl river on our return trip we again passed through a very rich and fertile country, and the enemy again became troublesome by occasionally making a dash on the rear guard or picking up some of the stragglers, but not materially retarding the progress of the army.

One poor fellow strayed a little from a foraging party; was caught by some bush-whackers, who cut off his ears and nose and otherwise mutilated him, then let him go. His head was badly swollen when he reached us, and he died a few days later.

We again crossed the Pearl river near Canton where we rested two days, during which time the boys of our regiment raked in a cotton wagon full of peanuts, some 50 fat turkeys, and an enormous amount of sweet potatoes, and we had quite a jolly time.

During our return trip there had come to us about 2000 white refugees and several thousand negroes, bringing along with them mules, cows, ox teams and whatever of earthly goods they could hastily gather together in their great desire to get out of rebellion into the land of the free. Many of them did not know where they were going, yet had an idea that the yankees were going to make them free and they mast follow the yankees. These made a caravan about ten miles long, and a motley looking crowd they were. It made me think of the Israelites coming out of Egypt with their kneading troughs on their backs. Men, women and children, fathers, mothers, children and grand-children, all trudged along beside the wagon each carrying an enormous pack on his back.

We used to tell them some glowing stories of what there was up in the northern country, which we told them was God's country, and the way their eyes would shine when they thought of that place where the darkies all were free, and how eagerly they would ask "Are yer guine up dar soon?" and "Can I go up dar too?"

With this immense train we also brought in about two thousand prisoners and a vast amount of forage, had destroyed millions of property, all the railroads in that part of the country, and had lost in killed, wounded, and missing, less than two hundred men. This was a decisive blow, and one from which I think the Confederacy never fully recovered.

VACATION

We arrived at Vicksburg on the 5th of March, and all who had reenlisted took steamers north on their leave of absence for 30 days. When we left Vicksburg, all was green as in summer. The peach trees were in full bloom, and even the mosquitos began to get saucy. At Cairo farmers were beginning to plow, and at Chicago it seemed as though we had struck mid-winter again.

On our arrival at Cairo we took the Illinois Central and passing up that road, many of the boys forgot they were again in "God's Country," and when the train would stop at a small town they would go into stores and help themselves to whatever they wanted as though they were in the enemies country and 'twas a necessity of war. Our bulky Uriah would rush into a saloon when the train would stop, call for a liquor, then take the bottle and glasses and start for the train. In this way many of the boys got "full" of the vile stuff, and I confess I began to be ashamed of the crowd. The inhabitants did not cheer us or build bon fires as they did on the way down three years before; but on our arrival at Bloomington the home of Company I the citizens turned out en mass and speeches were made on the public square and the ladies gave us a fine dinner.

From this place the boys began to scatter; we had turned over our arms at Springfield, and each sought his home to spend a season with his friends. I reached Chicago, and as I have said before, the snow blew and the chilly winds reminded one of the sunny south of Greenland, but when I reached Buffalo 'twas simply horrible. I had to wallow through the snow drifts many feet deep to reach my friends. I had a pleasant time for a few weeks at my old home but that time was all too short. Having been petted and fed like a spoiled child, I again went back to Chicago, then down to La Salle, then down the Central to Springfield where our Regiment was again being collected preparatory to again "going on the war path."

PART VI

An End In Sight

RETURNING TO THE FRONT

The boys arrived promptly on time, and quite a number of recruits were added to our ranks. We were quartered in the barracks of Camp Butler. Here our particular friend, Uriah, had several fights in which he got well battered by some Missouri boys.

Arriving at Cairo we received new arms and equipments and proceeded up the Ohio as far as Paducah, where we remained a few days and gave our recruits some thorough drill; then we passed up the Tennessee on transports as far as navigation would allow landing below the mussel shoals at Juka. Here we lay for several days while an immense herd of beef cattle were collected which we were to guard on their way to Georgia for Sherman's Army. Then we began a long march through Tennessee and Northern Alabama until we again reached the main army in Georgia.

Our long march was without any particular feature of interest. With our great herd of cattle we had to move slow. The weather was now delightful, and the roads good, and passing over the new country with summer's verdure was quite delightful. At Polaske, Tenn., we left our cattle to be forwarded by rail, and moved on to Huntsville, Alabama, where we rested a day, during which time Neals Olsen and I went into one of the large caves in the mountains with lighted candles, about half a mile, but after spending an hour in wandering around in the cold damp earth, was glad to get out of the dismal hole.

No enemy troubled us on our march, but as we crossed a river on an old ferry which was drawn over by a rope, the old thing sank and left the whole 20th Regiment floundering in the water of that murky stream, and for a time there was a scrabble for dear life, and John McEowen our Captain, came near being drowned, but was fished out by the boys. Then in crossing another river where there was no bridge we did not stop to build one, but stripped off our clothes, held them above water on our guns, and waded through the stream up to our necks to the other side, when we dressed and reformed. It was a long and tedious job to get the mule teams up the Allegheny mountains, and both men and beasts suffered greatly for the want of water. Yet upon the high table lands we found some delightful country, and here and there were little villages surrounded with green fields and groves of fruit, to which the boys helped themselves and vowed they would make that region their home "when this cruel war was over."

It was not until the 8th of June that we came within the sound of Sherman's guns, and we began to think that there was work ahead. It had now been a long time since we had heard the booming of cannon, and scarcely a gun had been fired on our march unless to shoot a hog, so the distant thunder of artillery reminded us of old times. The fighting we did not dread so much as the prospect of being cut off from our supplies and having to endure hunger as well as the hard work now before us, and when we neared the army we found that supplies were being brought forward on pack mules, and on seeing which the boys all shouted starvation.

Our own two divisions under Blair had but one load of "hard tack" left, not enough for a box to the company, which would give each man one or two crackers each for night and morning. So when 'twas quite dark we employed our "fighter" Uriah Henderson, who by the way was good at "jay hawking" to bring us a supply.

Going to the wagon which was closely guarded, he walked boldly past the sentinel with hand up and never stopped when he called "halt" but gruffly said "You tend to your business and I'll tend to mine." Then shouldering a box walked off with it leaving the sentinel to speculate as to whether it was the Commander in Chief or the President of the United States.

We crossed the Coosa River near Rome, after the enemy had evacuated that place, and united with the main army in the vicinity of Burnt Hickory and took our position in the 17th Army Corps on the 8th of June. Here we had some heavy skirmishing, but succeeded in pressing the enemy back to Ackworth, and from thence step by step until we reached Big Shanty, which is simply a railroad station with a few houses scattered around.

KENNESAW MOUNTAIN

From Big Shanty, the ground descends to a low plain which stretches back 3/4 of a mile, back of which rises the Kennesaw mountain, which forms the apex of a chain of mountains with Lost Mountain on the right and Pine Mountain on the left connected by a low range of foot hills called Black Jack.

On these mountains the whole Confederate Army under Johnston were concentrated to make a desperate stand. They had now been pushed back step by step from every strong position they had chosen and fortified from Chattanooga to this point, more than 200 miles and nothing would save the heart of the Confederacy but an immediate check of the National Forces on this side of the Chattahoochee. This position was as important as it was strong. Behind this position was Marietta and all the bridges and ferries leading to Atlanta the center of their manufactories and railway system in that part of the State.

On the tops of these mountains they had their signal stations; and all along the sides we could see their bristling cannon. Besides they had thoroughly entrenched themselves and seemed to bid defiance to any force that could be sent against them.

On the morning of the 10th of June our entire Army was drawn up in front of Big Shanty with McPherson on the left, Thomas in the Center and Schofield on the right, with General McCook looking to the rear and Gerrard's and Stoneman's cavalry on the flanks. General Sherman surrounded by his staff and corps commanders rode out in front and were in earnest conversation for more than two hours. We could see that the question of what next to do was a hard one to solve. A very Gibraltar was before us. To pass the mountain range without an enemy to confront would be hard indeed. But with a determined foe and hundreds of guns looking down on us, who but Billy Sherman would think of the thing?

But we made a general advance all along the line that very day skirmishing heavily at every point, driving back or capturing their outposts, and by night we were well up to the base of the mountains with nearly a thousand prisoners.

On the morning of the 11th being well up to the enemy disposition was made to break his line between Pine and Kennesaw mountains. We made a heavy assault on their works, but found them too strong. General Thomas moved his corps up the steep side of the Kennesaw, but the enemy easily repulsed him by rolling huge stones down on his men. Then a tremendous cannonade was kept up for several days during which the rebel General Polk was killed and several of their guns dismounted. By this time the large bridge across the Coosa had been completed and trains came rumbling up to Big Shanty laden with supplies. Sherman had an engine detached and run it close up to the enemy's line, a whistling all the way. They tried hard to hit the intruder but she got back all right, for which the brave engineers got leave of absence for 30 days.

On the 15th Pine Mountain was found to be abandoned by the enemy, when we made a forward move and got possession of a long line of entrenchments to the left extending along the Nick Jack Hills. From this elevated position we could see they had fortified a new line of defence, with wings thrown back near Marietta and Center on Kennesaw.

We could also look down on our former camps and see all the movements of troops in our rear, and on the 15th, we had a splendid view of a battle which was going on at our left, between Gerrards and the enemies Cavalry.

On the 17th Sherman ordered another assault made on the right center, when Lost Mountain was found to be abandoned together with another long line of entrenchments, and from this on we pressed hard upon the enemy at all points, skirmishing in dense forests or over impassable ravines, some of which engagements would have been considered heavy battles the first year of the war.

From their height on Kennesaw they could look down on our lines and see every move we made; hence we had to be extremely cautious and operate mostly at night.

All this time the rain came down in torrents rendering a general move next to impossible; yet a continual skirmish was kept up at all points, we pressing up as close to their works as possible, while the shell from their heavy guns would pass harmlessly over our heads. While here the boys ran out of tobacco, and no sutlers were allowed on this campaign; and nothing was transported by rail but army supplies; they had no means of obtaining the much coveted weed, and those who had long been addicted to its use suffered much, and would fill their mouths with the bark from roots of trees, bitter leaves or whatever would supply the passion for something to chew.

On the 22nd our line was advanced on the left when the enemy sallied forth, drove back our pickets, but when they reached our line of battle, received such a repulse that they hastily fled, leaving their dead and wounded on the field, with many provisions.

On the 27th of June, Sherman arranged for an assault to be made at two points on their works by General McPherson and Thomas at the left of Kennesaw. Accordingly our Corps made a detour of little Ken during the forepart of the night, and lay in the woods until morning close up to their pickets. Early the next morning we were in motion, drove in their out posts after a sharp fight, captured some prisoners and pushed close up to their main works, but halted under cover of some timber, where we lay flat down on the ground and let their artillery belch away at us for about two hours, but did not attempt to carry their works. The day was very warm and 'twas not so bad a thing to lay in the shade, but a hundred shells tearing around over our prostrate bodies was not altogether pleasant. I remember how a twelve pounder struck a large oak a little to our rear, then came bounding back to where we lay, as it rolled towards us I hit the thing with my foot and sent it back, but as luck would have it, it did not explode. The boys wanted to know if I had commenced a game of foot ball. It seemed that 'twas not in the program to storm their works at the point where we were, but to make a heavy demonstration to attract attention, while a strong effort was made at another point. So when our object was accomplished we withdrew, bringing our dead and wounded with us. In this engagement our Generals McCook and Harker were killed, and I think the attempt a failure as our aggregate loss was nearly 3,000 while we inflicted comparatively little harm on the enemy behind his secure fortifications.

On the night of July 1st, our whole Corps was relieved from in front of Kennesaw, and ordered to move to the right and threaten Nickajack Creek and Turners Ferry across the Chattahoochee. We moved in the darkness with the utmost caution. Not a sound was to be made; not a loud word spoken as we moved down past that long line of entrenchments all that night. In the morning we were a long way to the south of Lost Mountain, when we swung around in the direction of Nickajack Creek. Here we rested a while after our all nights march and tried in vain to obtain a little to eat; but all to no purpose. Our trains had not arrived, and we were far from our base of supplies.

With some heavy skirmishing our right was advanced down Nickajack, and we came upon the enemy strongly entrenched near Smyrna Church. In the meantime Johnston finding his left was being turned had evacuated Kennesaw and fell back to the line of the Chattahoochee and General Thomas had occupied Marietta and was falling upon the rear of the retreating army.

During these movements we would occasionally find time to slip away from the army on a little foraging expedition, especially when we would become tired of our hard tack and bacon. On the 3rd of July I slipped off in company with Joseph Getold and Russell Gowdy with our guns; traveled a long way down powder creek to where we thought the soldiers had not been, until we came to a good settlement, when we pitched in. We shot three sheep, a calf, some geese, and filled a large sack with new potatoes from an old lady's garden, and were ready to return with our plunder. But on collecting our forage we could not carry the half of it. What was to be done? It looked too tempting to leave; and there was not a horse, mule, or ox, to be found in all the neighborhood. We sat down to rest and meditate. Presently we heard the low rattle of wheels way up that country road. We listened, then peeked through the bushes, and could see an old man coming in an open buggy. He looked like a country parson or a Methodist circuit rider. We yanked our plunder out of sight in the bushes and concealed ourselves. When the buggy was within a few feet of our ambuscade, Russ Gowdy jumps out and leveling his gun at the old man shouts, "Halt!" The old man stops his horse as though shot and begins to tremble. We come up on both sides with bayonets fixed. "I'm a good peaceable citizen," says the old man. "I never took up arms against the Government in all me life. I. . ." "We don't care a continental what you are, or who you are. We want that old horse and buggy mighty quick," says Getold.

Glad to get off so easily, the old man rolled out and we piled the old rickety thing full to over-flowing, when Gowdy led the horse while Getold and I act as an escort back to camp.

The 4th of July was spent in heavy skirmishing around Smyrna Church in which we captured an entire line of the enemies pickets in their pits and becoming alarmed at their reverses on Nickajack fell back to the line of the Chattahoochee covering the crossings with strong fortifications.

We moved up in front of their position at Turners Ferry which was back of a large open field, and had to dodge their cannon ball all one day as they hurled them back at us in rapid succession. We tried all sorts of maneuvers to dislodge them from the ferry, going down the stream and firing at random to make them believe we were endeavoring to cross below, but they still held out, and we did not move them in the least. That night I was on picket duty, and when darkness had come on and the heavy guns had ceased their firing, I was sent with six chosen men a (vidit) to watch any move the enemy might make during the night.

We crawled, under cover of darkness, to about mid-way between the contending parties; and there concealed ourselves as best we could, in a clump of bushes, to await developments. About 12 o'clock they came out on their works with a band of music, and played a number of stirring airs, as though different bodies of troops were arriving; then they made a salley in considerable force, yelling and firing volleys of musketry to which our own men replied gallantly, and the balls riddled the bushes we were in, while we crouched close to the ground not daring to raise a head until the storm was over; besides it was so dark we could not find our way, or distinguish friend from foe. However, we held our ground until break of day, when to our surprise we found the "Rebs" had fled. Their demonstration during the night was but a feint to attract our attention while they were getting everything across the river. We shouldered our guns and marched back to our lines as big as life, never looking back to see if they were shooting at us or not. Most of the boys lay yet on the ground rolled up in their blankets fast asleep, but the few that were astir, looked at us with astonishment as if wondering at our boldness in easy range of the enemy. We quickly informed them that we had licked the whole crowd and run them across the river. Then we hastily communicated the intelligence to the commanding General, and in less than five minutes our line was in motion, and we were in undisputed possession of all north of the Chattahoochee.

The troops had now worked hard for many days and needed rest; so the time from the 10th to the 16th was spent in washing our clothes in the streams, picking the blackberries that grew to the size of a hens egg along the Chattahoochee bottom, or lounging idly around our camps. About twice each week our mail would arrive (which was always a large one). First to District Headquarters, then Regimental, then a Sergeant would receive his Company mail, mount a stump while the eager crowd would gather around him, each holding up his hand and yelling "here" long before he knew whether he was a lucky man or not. Then the Sergeant would call the name and drop the letter into the lucky one's hand. When all was fed the noise would cease, and some would go away grumbling, and others would find a lonely spot and eagerly drink in the contents of their missive from home.

During all this time vast stores were being collected at Altoona, Marietta and at other points convenient, and the cavalry were making, reconnaissance far down and across the river to create a diversion in that direction.

CROSSING THE CHATTAHOOCHEE

On the 17th all was in readiness for another forward move. General Thomas was to cross at Powers and Prices ferries. Schofield had already pushed a part of his command across at Soap Creek and marched out to Cross Keys, while McPherson was to transfer his command from the vicinity of Nickajack Creek on the right, to the extreme left and cross about 20 miles above in the vicinity of Roswell, then move directly east of Decatur and strike the Augusta Railroad near Stone Mountain. After two days of hard marching we came to the place of crossing where our pioneers had constructed a rude bridge of poles and unhewn timbers 30 feet above the water, which looked as though it might tumble as soon as we were on it.

All day long the 17th Army Corps was being hurried across this bridge and we poured southward in the direction of Decatur like a great army of locusts, filling forests, field and road. On the night of the 19th of July we bivouaced near the little town of Decatur, and in the morning moved due west along the line of the railroad in the direction of Atlanta. I do not remember that any part of the Army stopped to destroy anything. I know for ourselves, we hardly had time to eat, but on all the time from daybreak in the morn until dark, we were after the "Rebs" with a sharp stick and had no time for side issues. By five o'clock we had formed a junction with the left of Schofield's corps in the vicinity of Peach Tree Creek and face to face with the enemy which set up a hideous yell which extended it seemed for miles in each direction. Then our division was "double-quicked" to the left to prevent a flank movement, should the fighting begin.

BATTLE OF ATLANTA

On the night of the 20th we lay upon our arms in a thicket of scrub-oak in easy range of the enemy. A skirmish line was thrown out in our front, who during the night had thrown up some light breastworks to protect themselves, as the enemy's bullets were constantly whistling through the timbers in close proximity to our heads. The night was not long, though we did not sleep much; a few cat naps as our tired bodies lay stretched on the ground was all, then the gray streaks of dawn could be seen in the east, and as the light increased the pop-pop of guns in our front became more frequent and more and more annoying. I had a small tomato can attached to my belt, which I filled with water from my canteen, then gathering a few sticks lit them and proceeded to make a little coffee over the tiny fire while we were yet in line of battle. I did not succeed, for a bullet came spinning through the timber, put out my little fire and spilled what water I had left. As the light increased so that objects became more distinct in the thicket, the saucy minnies began to fly thicker and faster and we now stood in great danger of being hit, yet every soldier thought more of getting a little coffee or a few bites of "hard tack" than any thing else. But 'twas little use to try to take our morning meal in peace. The enemy lay in front of us about ten rods, their pickets five. They had worked all night like beavers and had thrown line upon line of breastworks.

It is now fairly light. Every man grasps his gun more tenaciously than before. "For God's sake, lets get at them" shouts one. 'Tis the sentiment of each. When soon the command forward was given. The line advances like a wall of fire. We scale our breastworks and move over an open field in solid column towards them, and John Norris is the first one to fall out of our own Company. We press on right up to their trenches under a withering fire from the enemy, then we halt and give them the best we have, and engage in a hand to hand conflict. For a time they stand fast and fight like tigers, but we gradually move them back and get possession of their breastworks. A part of our line goes over, but are soon forced back. We then fight across their works almost hand to hand for a long time, when Hood to recover the ground he had lost on this part of the field, sent up reinforcements who came down on us with a rush in solid column, and for a time the carnage was fearful. Our men sheltered themselves on the outside of the low breastworks, but they were getting an enfilading fire on us which swept the rear as well as the front of the works. Besides the small arms, shell were bursting every few minutes in our midst; and the shrieks of the men as they would have an arm or a leg shot off was terrible. It was now becoming a perfect slaughter pen for our men, yet we held on tenaciously to the ground we had gained, and I could see by looking along the line, that 'twas being paid for at a dear rate.

At this critical moment, I was ordered by our Colonel, to take six men and go to the right of the regiment, and try and drive off some "rebs" who were doing much execution on our right flank. We sprang forward, but before we reached the head of the regiment, I was struck with a minnie ball which passed completely through the right shoulder completely shattering and rendering that important member helpless. It did not bring me to the ground as is generally the case when one is hit with a minnie ball, nor cause much pain; a burning was all I felt in the excitement at the time; but the hot blood flowed so fast I soon sank to the ground and managed to crawl back from the line about five rods and could go no farther from loss of blood. I was then picked up by the Ambulance Corps and taken back into an open field where the wounded were being collected and being cared for by the surgeons. They had stretched a large piece of canvass across a pole which afforded us a partial shelter from the burning sun, and I knew little more of what was going on until the bullets began to cut their way through our tent, and raising my head a little, I could see the army wagons going for dear life around to the right, and the Ambulances were driven up to where we lay, and we were thrown in two or three deep and driven rapidly off over logs and stone, so that if our injuries were bad, they were made worse by this inhuman treatment. But this was essential to save us from falling into the hands of the enemy, and we could blame no one for our rough usage. A division of Hoods army had made a detour of our lines and came up in the rear of our left center compelling our men to fight them front and rear at the same time.

On the 22nd the fight was renewed with even greater fury than on the previous day, and neither side gaining any decided advantage. My own 20th Illinois was nearly annihilated. They fought desperately, but were surrounded and what were not killed were taken prisoners, and what few that were not in the fight went on with Sherman to the sea as mounted infantry. I lost in that battle two of my best friends, Russell Gowdy and Neals Olsen.

HOSPITAL IN THE WOODS

On the morning of the 22nd, I found myself on the ground in the woods surrounded on all sides by the wounded and the dying; attended by a few soldiers such as are generally found in the rear and are good for little else. We lay in this timber perhaps two weeks, during which time many had died. The boys managed to make us some rude bunks out of poles and boards so we was raised a little from the ground, but the things were so hard, we preferred rather the ground to having our bones prick through skin against the soft side of a board. A young man lay next to me who was so badly shot in the back that he had to lay face downwards for two weeks, and his constant cry of pain was truly pitiable. Finally the boys went to work and gathered a large amount of leaves; filled grain bags and made us quite comfortable beds. All this time I was too weak to walk or help myself, but I did not get lonesome for a young man of my company would come to my cot many times each day - with his face all disfigured by an ugly wound - and sit and tell the most ridiculous yarns so that those within hearing would have to laugh if there was any life in them, and he would get to laughing himself that he would burst the wound all open in his face. One fellow used to come around who had lost an arm, and used to declare that a man with one arm was the biggest liar on the face of the earth, and he said he expected to have to lie his way through the world, and one morning he came around early and with a solemn face said that he had discovered that the soup they was feeding us on was made in the great caldron kettle in the ravine by boiling up old secesh blankets that had not been washed since the war began. My watch (the one I have to this day) was all this time in my vest pocket into which the blood had run and completely coated the thing with black, as I had not had a change of clothing since the day of the battle and everything was in a terrible condition. Finally the more severely wounded were moved back across the river to Marietta, which journey I made laying in the bottom of a government wagon over a very rough road, and I think it was about as severe a journey as I ever took, for 'twas fearful to have such a jolting and shaking and the greatest wonder is I ever stood it to reach Marietta. That night I lay on the ground just where I was taken out of the wagon with nothing but a rubber blanket under me. In the morning the one that attended my wound counted twenty-four pieces of bone that had come out during the night.

Marietta was crowded with wounded soldiers; they had been brought back from all parts of the army, and every available space was occupied and their number was among the thousands. A committee from the Sanitary Commission was here who seemed very attentive and sympathetic on all occasions, and from them I obtained my first change of clothing when the old ones were cast off and burned. After staying at Marietta four or five days we were again moved back to

R O M E.

A train had been fitted up on purpose to transport the wounded, with beds and medicines and a corps of nurses, but as usual 'twas over-crowded and not enough help to attend to all, yet it came the nearest to comfort of anything I had seen since leaving the north.

On board this train I was placed and we were all day in making the short run. My arm had now begun to swell to double its natural size, turned black, and the surgeon in charge of the train said he was afraid it would have to be amputated.

At Rome our quarters were in large tents, provided with army cots on which was spread leaf mattresses. The buildings had all been filled previous to our arrival, and the town had become one vast hospital. I grew rapidly worse, my swollen arm had become almost unbearable, yet there was so much to do there, the nurses and surgeons were so busy, 'twas two days before I could get my wound dressed or the least attention paid to it. Finally I got the war surgeon at it, but while he was engaged in examining and dressing it the Surgeon-in-Chief came in and pronounced it Erysipelas and ordered me sent to the Erysipelas Ward. I told him I had not got it, and did not wish to expose myself to it. To which he sneeringly replied "I did not know anything about it." But the ward surgeon rather thought I was right and promised he would not have me moved for a while at least. The next morning the case was decided in my favor, for the wound broke open and discharged an incredible amount of pus, which together with a lance at the elbow greatly reduced its size and proved it to be an abscess. By this heavy drain on the system I was reduced to a mere skeleton and became too weak to raise my head and had to be fed with a spoon. The weather was very damp and sultry and the great green flies of Georgia became a source of great annoyance. They would hover around our cots in great swarms, and the least spot of blood or matter would soon be crawling with maggots. These were my greatest annoyance, and it makes me shudder even now to think of it. I was too weak to keep the flies away, and I could not have a nurse by me all the time, and I actually believe that for several mornings there were great white maggots enough taken from under my wound to fill a four quart measure.

There were no cases of slight wounds here. All had been severely hurt; consequently the death rate was very large. The gangrene set in during the warm weather, and the sufferings of those afflicted was terrible until death came to their relief. On the whole, Rome was the most gloomy place I was ever in, and was heartily glad when I got well enough to be moved away. After a while I gained sufficient strength to stand on my feet and walk by holding on to something. Then I began to long for the water, and slipping off one day unperceived by the guard, went to the Coosa River about twenty rods distant and let myself into that rapidly flowing stream and kept myself from floating down by hanging on to some bushes that grew on its banks. I remained in the water a long time and finally crawled back to my cot dripping wet. This done me good, my appetite became voracious, and 'twas hard to get enough to eat. I rapidly gained strength and was soon able to walk about the town with my arm in a sling as well as the best of them. In September I was granted leave of absence for 30 days and with a little satchel walked down to Kingston six miles to catch a train going north. They did not run on schedule time and when a train came along made up of platform cars, I jumped on board fearing 'twould be my only chance. All night long I lay on my back on the hard platform in the open air and was jolted and shook and shook and jirked, with a cloud of smoke and cinders blinding my eyes and filling my clothes and skin with clouds of soot and ashes.

Oh war'nt I glad when I reached Chattanooga. There I went directly and bought three or four pies intending to partly make a meal on those, but when I got back to the depot the Hospital train had arrived and meeting the Surgeon in charge he told me if I would throw away my pies and put on the sick suit, he would give me some breakfast fit to eat and a passage to Nashville. I gladly slung my "sole leather" pies into the ditch and donned the required suit and had a comfortable passage to Nashville. This I might have had all the way if I had had a little patience to wait. Next day I took the regular passenger for Louisville and reached Chicago a few days later, and was quartered over night in the dirty rickety Old Soldiers Home on the Lake Front.

When my leave expired I reported back as far as Louisville, where I was examined by the Army Surgeons and was pronounced unfit for duty and was quartered in Clay Hospital.

CLAY HOSPITAL

This was a large brick building, formerly used as a female college named in honor of Henry Clay, but when the war broke out was converted into a hospital. It was a commodious building, admirably fitted up, everything clean and comfortable with a good and efficient corps of nurses.

I was now away from all whom I knew, but soon became acquainted with others, and the time passed most pleasantly during my stay of two months. The ladies too were extremely kind to the disabled boys and it seemed they could not do enough for us. They were constant visitors, bringing books and papers to read, often giving entertainments; besides we had access to a large library furnished by the loyal people of the city. 'Tis true, some of the boys were unruly, and would steal pies out of the pantry, would tease the girls when they came to scrub the floors - the penalty for such offenses was always two days in bed - yet as a rule the utmost good order prevailed.

We had no need to steal chickens, for they came to us without the asking; and on Christmas the ladies eclipsed all attempts at dinner with the bountiful one they gave us in the great auditorium. But the time soon came when we had to be removed from these delightful quarters, to make room for those who were constantly arriving from the front. Accordingly a steamer was loaded with about 500 of those who were so badly disabled as to be of no further use to the front; and started down the Ohio about the first of February 1865. We were many days on the water with the weather cold and stormy and the river full of floating ice which made our progress slow. For a time the officers of the boat tried hard to keep the crowd out of the cabin compelling them to weather the storm and sleep as best they could on deck amid packages of freight. After passing one cold gloomy night on deck, we organized to make a raid on the upper part of the boat, and if necessary throw the crew overboard. When they found we were determined they yielded and we had the warm fires of the cabin to ourselves, and on nights the floors would be so completely covered with sleeping soldiers, it was next to impossible to move around. This crowded condition was most disagreeable and caused much suffering during our trip of five days; two or three of the boys died and others were made seriously ill. My old friend Ed Smith was along, the only one from the 20th Regiment, in fact the only one that I had with me that I knew until the close of the war. It was a happy time for us when we left that old boat now covered with filth and went on shore at

JEFFERSON BARRACKS.

The Barracks was not now a regular military post, but one vast hospital covering many acres. The old barracks were of stone forming three sides of a square enclosing a beautiful piece of ground where Uncle Sam had trained his young men for war.

When John C. Fremont was in command of the west, he had caused to be erected around the inner circle an outer row of wood buildings which more than doubled their former capacity.

Smith and I were assigned to a convalescent ward next to the big square by the river banks; (lucky for us). The surgeon in charge was badly crippled by an explosion, earthquake or something terrible, for one of his legs were as crooked as a ram's horn and did not reach half way to the ground, and dangled like a shirt on a bean pole as he flew up and down the ward on his two crutches. His favorite prescription for most everything was invariably "Ferry Compound" hence we called him Ferry, as I did not know his real name. Ferry was a good fellow and I stood well in with him, and it was amusing to see him make his rounds of a morning. If a man was having a chill, he would quickly say, "Ferry Compound." If a fever, 'twas Ferry Compound. In all cases where medicines were to be taken 'twas Ferry Compound. If the gangrene had set into a wound and had to be burned out, Ferry would tell the nurse to "burn it all it needed; then be sure and burn it a little more." He was extremely fond of music, would bring his melodian into the ward, and play and sing for hours thinking perhaps 'twould have the same soothing effect as Ferry Compound.

There was also a middle aged female who had a room at the far end of the ward, whom the boys called "mother." Mother was about 35, tolerable good looking, though what she had ever done to merit her title, I never could see; yet the boys all liked her and one day gave her a present of a purse of $30 to which she responded in a rousing speech at the lower end of the hall.

But the trouble with mother was she liked company, and much of the sanitary wine and other delicacies found its way to her room without the boys getting a smell.

We had a fine lodge of I.O. of G.T. which used to meet once a week in a vacant building where the lame, the halt would congregate, together with a goodly number of young ladies from the surrounding country, for a general good time. Mother was chief cook in this as was also the matrons from several of the other wards. We came before the public in a fine exhibition. The Hall was packed at twenty-five cents a head, and what became of the money was quite a mystery to us all.

During the winter another abscess formed on my arm and I again became quite ill, and had to be removed from the convalescent to the Erysipelas ward, where there were about twenty down with the latter disease. Ferry was in charge here also. He had shaved the heads of his patients and plastered them with flour and glycerine, so they were a motley sight to behold; yet all were doing well under his care and felt fine, especially after receiving the usual allowance of grog. One would be known as "Pall Parrot" another as "Balled Eagle," "Merrills Horse" and so on, but Missouri Smith was the boy that could take the house down on a practical joke the best of any one in the crowd.

Well, I lay for about four weeks with my arm packed in a bag of dry flour - which by the way, served greatly to alleviate the pain - during which time I devoured several volumes of Dickens and counted myself happy with my pleasant surroundings; yet worrying a good deal by day and by night as to what I should do in the great outside world in my crippled condition, in which state I now plainly saw I must always remain. Together with my friend Smith I conjured up all sorts of schemes and we built many "castles in the air" which never materialized, as I never saw Smith again after leaving the Barracks.

As the warm weather of spring came on I had greatly improved. Was now able to take many a long walk to Carondelet and St. Louis, but my arm from its long confinement in a sling had grown stiff at the elbow, and 'twas a long time before I could get my hand down to my side.

After our walks and outdoor excercise, we would while away the rest of the day at chess, which was a favorite pass time here, and some times keep up our sport until the Dutch sentinel would come around crying, "Make dow the lights; after taps." Or if the sentinel had been a sailor he would shout, "Dows the glim after taps."

On the 15th of May I was a little surprised on the receipt by mail of my "final statement" and on its examination found I had been promoted since the battle of Atlanta to Orderly Sergeant which gave me much more pay than I had expected; but was still more surprised on opening another package to find from headquarters of Illinois a Commission of 1st Lieutenant of Co. "H" 20th Illinois signed by Governor Ogelsby. These papers came to me about the time of Lee's surrender of the Confederate armies of Virginia, and it was generally understood that the war was virtually over. Sherman's Army was on its way north from the Carolinas to attend the Grand Review at the Capital and would soon be on its way west and it was rumored that our Division (General Legget's) would be retained for duty on the frontier in Texas. If this should be so, I thought the best thing I could do was to rejoin my Regiment if I was able to serve as commissioned officer, as the pay would be much more than I could make in any other capacity. Besides, I felt a strong desire to see the boys once more, and be mustered out with them. So I then determined to meet them on their way from Washington.

I then applied and received my discharge as an enlisted man, drew my pay, and bidding my friends at the Barracks goodbye, especially Mother and Ferry, I left for Chicago, where I spent several days at the Great Sanitary Fair, went down and joined my old comrades at Louisville, Ky.

General Legget's Division were in camp about a mile from the city in a grove, and the soldiers had little to do but carouse around the town, and some of them I noticed, had become pretty hard characters.

After a few days I was mustered in as 1st Lt. of Co. "H" but had little to do save make out the final rolls of the Company, which took many days of hard work. The regiment was now in command of Harry King of Brittons Lane fame, who had passed from Corporal up through the different grades of rank to the head of the regiment; and the boys were quite proud of him.

After the famous "March to the Sea" we had received numerous accessions from Hospital, Southern Prisons and home, but with all these we did not muster but a little over five hundred, and many of these had received wounds or contracted diseases which rendered them unfit for soldiers.

We had no drills or parades now, and there was nothing to distinguish our camp from a lot of gypsies save the <u>guard mount</u> which was always done up in fine style. Once during our stay here I was chosen as officer of the Guard, and the only instructions from Headquarters I had was not to allow any whiskey brought into camp, but to confiscate all that was found. This was on the fourth of July and many of the boys had gone off to town and got pretty well filled up. One Dutchman came back and said he was bearer of twenty four glasses of beer all of which he stood on the outside of hence we could not confiscate the stuff.

At the gate it was not long before a troop of women came along (all Irish) bearing well filled baskets of apples, oranges, cakes, etc., to sell to the soldiers. The Sentinel of course halted them at the gate when I proceeded to examine them by asking what they had in their baskets?

"And shure ye'r a foine dacent man and can't ye see what me got in me basket wid yer own eyes?"

"Got any whiskey in the bottom of that basket?"

"Indad I haven't! Do ye think that the likes of me would be so mane as to bring whiskey up hare wen its agin the Ginerls orders?"

"Then I'll go to the bottom of your basket and see."

"Holy mother save us," as I run my hand down the side of her basket and brought out three or four flasks well filled with the "creature." Then I confiscated the entire contents of several baskets which furnished a great feast for the boys on guard, but the flasks under the instructions of the officer of the day I took to my tent intending to turn over to the headquarters as soon as off of duty. But having occasion to go up to my tent during the night, I heard the sound of voices within before I got there and stopped to listen, when I could hear their lips smack after a drink and say in a low voice: "A fine old rabbit. A fine old rabbit." My Captain and the adjutant had found the flasks and nearly devoured their contents.

The talk about going to Texas had nearly died out since the death of Maximilian in Mexico, but word was sent from Washington that those of the officers who wished commissions for the Regular Army would be examined and their applications sent on to the War Department. About twenty of us underwent a thorough examination and we each wrote out a statement of our military experience which was forwarded together with our examination, but that was the last we ever heard from it.

H O M E W A R D

We struck our tents for the last time on the 13th of July, 1865, and turned over our camp and garrison equipage to the government, went over to New Albany and took a train for Chicago, where we arrived on the 18th and were quartered at Camp Douglas, preparatory to being mustered out.

The boys did not stay at the camp much for it was a filthy place; but found accommodations in the different boarding houses in the locality, that our stay might be as agreeable as possible, and as some of them would say, to become accustomed to living in a house again.

I was busy with the final statements during our stay of a week here, but could not help contrast the difference between the regiment now, and what it was four years before. When we left Joliet we were a little over one thousand strong, all young and healthy men as ever went to the front. We had received over a thousand recruits; but now we have not an officer who went out with us in 61, and but few of the original men left. Some of these had grown gray, had contracted disease or received wounds which they would in all probability have to carry through life. We had also laid away many from hospital and field whose bones were now bleaching the southern soil, and the little band which were now left to bear our colors homeward, all tattered and torn in many battles, had spent four years of the best of their lives in their country's service, and were now physical wrecks of their former selves.

Yet we saw no reason to complain. He who goes as a soldier must take his chances. The Government had done nobly by us; clothing and feeding us well and paying every dollar that was our due. And what was better than all, we came home with the satisfaction that in this war we had done well our part, in conquering an honorable peace. We had seen the last armed foe submit to the rightful authority of the government, we had four millions of slaves made free, and our flag, the emblem of liberty, floating in triumph from the Atlantic to the Pacific, from the Lakes to the Gulf.

We deposited our battle flag with the Archives at the State Capital where the Regimental Rolls will be found. And on the 1st day of August 1865, disbanded, having been in the service four years and three months, when each man sought his home and the pursuit of happiness.

The End.

APPENDIX I

Twentieth Infantry Field Staff and Officers

Colonels
C. Carroll Marsh   Resigned April 22, 1863
Daniel Bradley   Discharged February 13, 1865
Harry King   M.O. as Lt. Col. July 16, 1865

Lt. Colonels
William Irwin   Killed at Ft. Donaldson,
                                       February 16, 1862
Evan Richards   Killed at Raymond, May 12, 1863
Danl. Bradley   Promoted to Colonel
Harry King   Promoted to Colonel

Majors
John W. Goodwin   Discharged Dec. 17, 1861
Evan Richards   Promoted to Lt. Colonel
F. A. Barletson   M.O. Aug. 30, 1862 in 100 Reg.
Danl Bradley   Promoted to Lt. Colonel
Geo. W. Kennard   Discharged Jan. 7, 1865
Roland Evans   M.O. July 16, 1865

Adjutants
Jno. E. Thompson   Killed at Shiloh, Apr. 6, 1862
Jno. R. Conklin   M.O. November 27, 1864
Frank Chester   M.O. July 16, 1865

Quartermasters
Jno. Spicer   Resigned
Joel H. Dix   Declined, not mustered
Bradford Church   Cancelled
Lysander Tiffany   M.O. July 16, 1865

Surgeons

Christopher Goodbrake	Resigned, Sept. 17, 1864
Rolla T. Richards	Promoted

1st Assistants

Fred K. Baley	Resigned Aug. 31, 1862
Rolla T. Richards	M.O. July 16, 1865

Chaplains

Chas. Button	Resigned Mar. 24, 1863
Saml Richards	Resigned Jan. 29, 1864

APPENDIX II

Company "H"

Name & Rank	Residence	Remarks
Captains		
Orton Frisbie	Granville	Dismissed for neglect of duty, Nov. 16, 1862
Victor H. Stevens	Tonica	Killed at Raymond, May 12, 1863
Jno. McEowen	Granville	M.O. July 16, 1865
1st Lieutenants		
Frank Whiting		Resigned Oct. 31, 1862
V. H. Stevens	Tonica	Promoted
Wm. Ware	Granville	Pro. in Sig. Corps Aug. 20, 1864
Ira Blanchard	La Salle	M.O. July 16, 1865
2nd Lieutenants		
John W. Powell		Pro. to Co. "F" 2nd Infantry
Wm. Ware	Granville	Promoted
Jno. McEowen	Granville	Promoted
Ephram Cassell	Florida	M.O. July 16, 1865 as Sergt.
Sergeant		
V.H. Stevens	Tonica	Promoted to 1st Lieut.
Sergeants		
Jno. McEowen	Granville	Pro.to 1st Sergt. & 2nd Lt.
Wm. Ware	Granville	Pro. to Q.M. Sergeant
Ira Blanchard	La Salle	Re-enlisted a Veteran
Saml. Forbes	Granville	Discharged July 23, 1862; wounds

Name & Rank	Residence	Remarks
Corporals		
Theo Margrave	Granville	Discharged June 13, 1864
DeWitt C. Higgins	Tonica	Killed at Ft. Donaldson
C. B. Champany	Peru	Discharged July 31, 1862; wounds
L. H. Smith	Granville	Discharged July 23, 1862
J. P. Albright	Hennepin	Discharged May 31, 1862; disability
Jno. Cunningham	Granville	Discharged July 21, 1862; wounds
Uriah Henderson	Florida	Discharged April 5, 1862; disabled
Moses L. Tullis	Peru	Discharges Nov. 20, 1861; disabled
Musicians		
Michael Hogan	Tonica	Discharged June 13, 1864
Benj. F. Harford	Tonica	Re-enlisted as Veteran
Wagoner		
Lars Olsen	Granville	Discharged Oct. 14, 1861; disabled
Privates		
Agart, August	Hennepin	Re-enlisted as Veteran
Ashley, Norris J.	Magnolia	Died at Andersonville
Acklin, Geo. W.	Peru	Died at Andersonville
Bennett, Martin F.	Cedar Point	Discharged June 13, 1864
Bennett, Stephen	Cedar Point	Died Oct. 20, 1861
Buck, Noble H.	Tonica	Re-enlisted as Veteran
Cunningham, G. M.	Magnolia	Discharged July 11, 1862; wounds
Crane, Solomon	Vermilions-ville	Discharged Nov. 6, 1861; disability

Name & Rank	Residence	Remarks
Cassell, Ephram	Florida	Re-enlisted as Veteran
Cassell, Henry	Florida	Discharged June 13, 1864
Cassell, Calvin	Florida	Discharged Nov. 26, 1861; disability
Clark, Lucius K.	Magnolia	Died March 17, 1862
Cook, Jno. M.	Baynes Point	Discharged Feb. 3, 1862; disabled
Dixon, Francis M.	Cedar Point	Killed at Shiloh, April 6, 1862
Darrah, Robert	Granville	Killed at Raymond, May 1862
Davis, Robert	Florida	Discharged June 13, 1864
Forbs, William	La Salle	Died May 24, 1863; wounds
Folsom, Nathan	Peru	Discharged Jan. 19, 1863
Folsom, Horatio Q.	Peru	Discharged Aug. 11, 1862; wounds
Gilmer, Allen	Peru	Died March 12, 1862; wounds
Gowdy, Russell	Hennepin	Killed at Atlanta, July 22, 1864
Getold, Joseph	Hennepin	Discharged June 13, 1864
Henderson, Isaac	Florida	Discharged Oct. 12, 1862; wounds
Hamilton, John	New London	Transferred to Gunboat 1862
Hardy, Sylvanus	Vermilion	Re-enlisted as Veteran
Jetter, Geo. S.	Hennepin	Killed at Raymond, May 12, 1863
Jahle, George	Granville	Discharged June 13, 1864
Jewill, Washington	Lowell	Discharged Nov. 28, 1862; disability
Julian, Thomas	Tonica	Discharged July 23, 1862; wounds
Keep, Jno. O.	Tonica	Discharged July 23, 1862; wounds
Lane, Chas. H.	Granville	Discharged Oct. 12, 1861; disability
Lighthart, Calvin	Magnolia	M.O. June 13, 1864

Name & Rank	Residence	Remarks
Milliken, Oscar	Tonica	Transferred to Signal Corps
McEowen, Benj.	Granville	Discharged July 27, 1862; disability
McEowen, Jno.	Granville	Killed at Ft. Donaldson
Molter, Amos	Tonica	Discharged Sept. 9, 1862; disability
McFusen, Alex	Tonica	Drowned Illinois River, Dec. 20, 1862
Mayo, Joseph R.	Mt. Paletine	Discharged June 13, 1864
Munday, Theo	Peru	Deserted Aug. 18, 1862
Murray, Tho.	Peru	Deserted Feb. 2, 1862
Nixon, Frank	Hennepin	Discharged Feb. 2, 1862
Olsen, Neals	Granville	Killed at Atlanta, July 22, 1864
Porter, Albert	Cedar Point	Re-enlisted as Veteran
Powell, Jno. W.	Hennepin	Promoted to Sergeant Major
Palmer, Geo. F.	Tonica	Discharged June 13, 1864
Roberts, Jno. C.	Granville	Died May 12, 1863; wounds
Rolstin, James	Hennepin	Re-enlisted as Veteran
Robinson, John	Tonica	Died at Tonica, May 19, 1862
Ross, Norman L.	La Salle Co.	Discharged June 13, 1864
Smith, Louis	Hennepin	Deserted April 5, 1862
Shelton, Abner J.	Cedar Point	Discharged June 13, 1864
Sehons, Henry	Peru	Died at Savannah, April 3, 1862
Schrider, Jno. H. D.	Tonica	Killed at Shiloh, April 6, 1862
Salyards, Marshall	Long Point	Transferred to Signal Corps
Scheffer, Conrad	Granville	Re-enlisted as Veteran
Simonton, Henry	Magnolia	Died at Mound City, Oct. 30, 1861
Slater, Hugh E.	La Salle	Discharged March 6, 1862
Van Husen, A. Duane	La Salle	Re-enlisted as Veteran

Name & Rank	Residence	Remarks
Walrath, Aaron A.	Tonica	Re-enlisted as Veteran
Whittaker, Albert E.	Granville	Died at Mound City, Oct. 21, 1861
Ward, Martin L.	Eagle	Discharged June 13, 1864

GLOSSARY

<u>abettis</u> (from the French word abatis) A defensive position represented by felled trees with their tops facing in the direction of the enemy. The branches were usually sharpened and acted as spikes which were to thwart an advance by opposing forces.

<u>ambuscade</u> 19th Century term for ambush.

<u>billy</u> "Billy Yank" was the common name given to every union soldier by the confederates. The Yankee equivalent for the southern soldier was "Johnny Reb."

<u>bivouacked</u> To make camp in a temporary manner, a soldier usually had little or no shelter.

<u>breastworks</u> Temporary fortifications.

<u>bum</u> A raucous jaunt with no specific purpose; hell-raising; a drinking spree.

<u>bush-wackers</u> Renegade soldiers who lived off of or in the woods. They were known to be corrupt, violent, and rarely answered to any real authority.

butternut A synonym for the Confederate soldier used late in the war. Many Southerners wore uniforms colored by a yellowish-brown dye made from copperas and walnut hulls.

cockade A decorative ornament worn on a hat as a badge.

corduroying The building of roads using logs which were laid down side by side. This same technique was used in the crossing of rivers and streams.

"corn pone" A staple of the southern diet, it was simply corn bread often made without milk or eggs and then fried.

echelon The arrangement of a body of troops with units somewhat to the left or to the right of the rear unit.

erysipelas Staff infection resulting in inflammation, intense local swelling, and high fever.

"Fight it out on that line if it did take all summer" A play on General Grant's comment in June of 1864 in which he reaffirms his intention to take control of Richmond despite his catastrophic losses. i.e. "I am going through on this line if it takes all summer."

gabions A gabion was used to reinforce fieldworks. Dating back to the 1640's and Oliver Cromwell, a gabion was a cylindrical wicker basket about three feet high and filled with stones and dirt.

grape and canister A discharge from an artillery piece. It consisted of a tin canister full of lead balls of varying weights. Used only at distances of about 250 yards or less, it was mainly an anti-personnel weapon which ripped into opposing ranks in a terrifying and destructive manner.

hard tack A staple of the Civil War soldier's diet. It was a 1/4 inch thick saltless biscuit made of flour and water.

<u>Hardin's tactics</u> Actually, Hardee's tactics. As Napoleonic tactics became obsolete, William J. Hardee, a Georgian born West Pointer, began work on a revised manual for soldiers on rifle and light infantry tactics in 1853. It addressed the changing conditions in battlefield tactics and made adjustments for the technological advances in weaponry. Hardee's tactics soon became the Bible for all officers, North and South. It should be noted that William J. Hardee was to become a Lt. General in the Confederate army.

<u>haversack</u> Similar to a knapsack but worn over the right shoulder. Usually about a square foot in size, it held the soldier's daily rations.

<u>hollow square</u> Strictly a defensive maneuver, the soldiers would position themselves in a large square to fend off opposing cavalry or infantry charges.

<u>keno</u> A form of gambling involving a string of five winning numbers similar to bingo.

<u>killickinnick</u> A specific brand of choice tobacco of the period.

<u>long roll</u> A lengthy continuous drum roll to signal alert or imminent danger.

<u>minnies</u> A hollow-based lead bullet of conical shaped developed around 1850 by Captain Claude Minie of the French army. The bullet would expand into the grooved bore of the rifle. Speed in loading the weapon, combined with greater accuracy, made this one of the significant technological advances during the Civil War period.

<u>"Old Abe"</u> Was the war eagle mascot of the 8th Wisconsin volunteers, not the 16th Wisconsin as stated by Blanchard. When the regiment went into battle, the bird would fly over the fighting, screeching at the enemy, and then return to his perch. The rebels made many attempts to shoot or capture him but to no avail. He died in 1881 of smoke inhalation when the capitol in Madison burned down.

paroled Captured prisoners were sometimes paroled, and allowed to go free on the condition that they took an oath not to fight again. The use of "parolling" became less frequent as the war went on.

pickets A detached body of soldiers sent out on the perimeter to guard the main force from a surprise attack. They would often exchange news with the enemy and trade in desirable products, i.e. coffee and tobacco.

Pittsburg Landing A Landing located on the west side of the Tennessee River. The Battle of Shiloh (named after Shiloh Church) is historically synonymous with the Battle of Pittsburg Landing. Northerners refer to if as the Battle of Pittsburg Landing and Southerners refer to it as the Battle of Shiloh.

redoubs A multi-sided extension of a permanent fortress, these redoubts were defensive works supporting a main fort or fortified line.

rod A measured distance equivalent to 16 1/2 feet; twenty rods equals just over 100 yards.

Rumt. fever (rheumatic fever) Severe infectious disease usually occurring in young adults characterized by painful swollen joints, fever, and inflamed heart lining.

secesh Union terminology for a rebel soldier or southern sympathizer; short for "secessionist."

sutler A civilian entrepreneur who followed and supplied armies with various items for sale. A soldier could purchase items such as food, newspapers, books, tobacco, razors, pots, pans, and illegal alcohol.

vidit (vedette) Soldiers stationed in advance of pickets to keep vigil on the enemy force and its movements.

wide awake Probable reference to some type of political "gopher" for Lincoln's 1858 Senatorial campaign.

INDEX